SPECIAL MESSAGE TO READERS

THE ULVERSCROFT FOUNDATION
(registered UK charity number 264873)
was established in 1972 to provide funds for
research, diagnosis and treatment of eye diseases.
Examples of major projects funded by
the Ulverscroft Foundation are:-

- The Children's Eye Unit at Moorfields Eye Hospital, London
- The Ulverscroft Children's Eye Unit at Great Ormond Street Hospital for Sick Children
- Funding research into eye diseases and treatment at the Department of Ophthalmology, University of Leicester
- The Ulverscroft Vision Research Group, Institute of Child Health
- Twin operating theatres at the Western Ophthalmic Hospital, London
- The Chair of Ophthalmology at the Royal Australian College of Ophthalmologists

You can help further the work of the Foundation
by making a donation or leaving a legacy.
Every contribution is gratefully received. If you
would like to help support the Foundation or
require further information, please contact:

THE ULVERSCROFT FOUNDATION
The Green, Bradgate Road, Anstey
Leicester LE7 7FU, England
Tel: (0116) 236 4325

website: www.foundation.ulverscroft.com

THE LATE MRS. FIVE

Soon after Paul Porter arrives in the small rural town of Lowndesburg, he is shocked to see his beautiful ex-wife Edith getting into an expensive limousine. He discovers she is now married to rich landowner John Hilliard the Fifth, to whose mansion he makes a visit hoping to sell agricultural machinery, only to find nobody home. But the local police know of his visit — and when they discover Edith's dead body there, he becomes the prime suspect as the slayer of the late Mrs. Five!

Books by Richard Wormser
in the Linford Mystery Library:

PERFECT PIGEON

RICHARD WORMSER

THE LATE MRS. FIVE

Complete and Unabridged

LINFORD
Leicester

First published in Great Britain

First Linford Edition
published 2018

A catalogue record for this book is available
from the British Library.

ISBN 978–1–4448–3765–0

Published by
F. A. Thorpe (Publishing)
Anstey, Leicestershire

Set by Words & Graphics Ltd.
Anstey, Leicestershire
Printed and bound in Great Britain by
T. J. International Ltd., Padstow, Cornwall

This book is printed on acid-free paper

1

I had always thought of this part of the United States as flat, like Kansas, or maybe Indiana, but it wasn't. You came over ridges where the trees had cones, needles and grew in nicely spaced rows, and then you went downhill and there were the hardwoods, the oaks and the maples and some others — maybe black walnuts — that I didn't know the names of. The leafy trees didn't grow as neatly as the evergreens, and the underbrush was thick amongst them, and little brooks ran to the road and under it in metal and stone culverts.

Then there was a valley, very green now in the spring, and some of the farms had wire fences and raised hogs, and others had whitewashed rail fences and raised horses and cows, but everybody raised corn; it was coming up bravely.

Everything was very fine-looking. I felt wonderful. The car was new and it was mine, but the mileage was the company's; and, at the rate I was running it out, the company was going to pay for a year's depreciation in a couple of months.

Cutting across the valley, I came to a split in the road; not a crossroads, but one of those federal highway splits: LOWNDES-BURG BUSINESS, and LOWNDESBURG BYPASS. There was a rig of ours in Lowndes-burg that had been unsold for quite a while; I had a card in my pocket from the boss about it. So I chose business and headed into town.

It seemed like an all right little town, although, in the manner of the midwest, they had cut down all the trees on the business streets. Two banks, a small hotel, three movie houses, a big department store and a smaller, classier one; a Chinese restaurant and three non-Chinese ones.

On a street paralleling the main drag, but two blocks nearer the railroad tracks, I found what I was looking for: J. F. Gray's Feed & Seed Co. had one of our terracers in the window. There was a woman in the front part of J. F. Gray's.

Out back, I could see men working on the loading platforms and in the sheds; hay and seed and barbed wire and hog wire were selling that day.

When I asked for the boss, she just looked up from the bills she was posting and said, 'Over in the jail, I think.' I must have looked surprised. She grinned. 'You're not one of the regular salesmen who call on us, are you? Don't be surprised — Dad's also chief of police.'

'Well, if you're part of the firm, maybe you can tell me what I want to know. I'm not a salesman; I'm a factory rep for that terracer you've got on display.'

She nodded and stood up. I was surprised at her height — about five feet seven — because it was mostly in her legs. Sitting down she had seemed quite a short woman, and I don't like short women particularly, maybe because I've had better luck with tall ones.

'I could tell you aren't a salesman,' she said. 'When I tell them Dad's the police department here, they always say something about having to watch their step.'

'Always?'

'Mostly. What do you want to know about the terracer?'

'Have you ever sold any of them? Do the owners like them? What objections have been made by people you've shown this one to?'

'I guess you'll have to talk to the boss, after all,' she said. 'I'm mostly the bookkeeper, telephone answerer and taker-of-orders. Offhand, though, I'd say you've got your machine in the wrong place. If a terracer does what I think it does, it's for hilly country. This is all flatland farming around here.'

She had moved over to the big swing-up window as she talked. Naturally I followed her, and we stood there, looking unintelligently at the leveler. She tapped a natural-polished fingernail on one of her front teeth and said, 'Tell me, why did you paint it blue?'

'Well, I'm working up to the paint department, but as I get it, the boss figured land-moving machinery's almost always red or yellow or orange. When people see one of ours, they remember it, and because it's doing a good job, we want them to remember it.'

'Who isn't a salesman?' she said, and then turned. 'Here's Dad now.' The smile she gave me as she went away was polite, no more.

I fished a card out of my pocket and advanced on Dad. About fifty, short and broad, with that facial resemblance to Harry Truman you find so often in small towns. 'Mr. Gray, I'm Paul Porter.'

He grunted, took the card, read it, and said, 'Well, all right, but I'm not Mr. Gray. He's my father-in-law. I'm Otto McLane.'

'Sorry. Mr. McLane, your daughter tells me you've had trouble moving our terracer because the land's too flat around here. Now that's just where we've done the most good. Most flatland farmers own the hills behind them, but they don't farm them because — well, because they're flatland farmers. With a terracer, we can reproduce flat conditions on a hillside, and maybe add a third to the arable acreage of the valley-edge farms.'

He was moving across the sales floor as

we talked. His daughter had gone back to her desk and her books. He patted her sleek hair once in passing and said, 'Any calls I ought to know about, Andy?'

She gave him her nice smile. 'Not if Bill got you.'

'Did. Gonna be a month late with his check. Told him it was fine. C'mon in my office, Mr. Porter. You interest me.' The office was three half-glass walls set up against the concrete block partition that backed on the loading dock. We sat down in the proper chairs, fished out our cigarettes, waggled them politely at each other, and then each lighted his own brand.

'Yep,' he said. 'You've got the picture wrong, but you interest me. Here's where you're wrong: our customers don't own the hills behind them. Here's where you interest me: the man who does own them is named John Hilliard Five, and he's got all the money in the world. Maybe you could sell him; I can't.'

I asked what Mr. Five did with his land.

'His name isn't Five, it's Hilliard; he's

6

the fifth of the name. And he rides horses on it. His dad, John Four, used to hunt on it; he doesn't even do that. Doesn't even bother to raise his own horse feed. Buys hay and grain from me. About my biggest customer.'

I started to say something when a frightful screaming drove the words out of my mouth. But Mr. McLane calmly pulled a thin gold watch out of his pocket and set it. 'Air raid siren,' he said. 'Use it at noon for a test.'

Feeling slightly foolish, I played to recover. 'May my expense account take you to lunch?'

'Sure.'

As we came out of the office, a boy was coming in from the loading dock. Andy McLane got up, saying something like, 'Right on time, Jim,' and started poking at her hair with her fingertips.

'I'm taking your father to lunch, Miss McLane. Be nice if you could join us.'

There was no coquette in her. She nodded, said, 'Give me two minutes,' and went through a door behind which a flash of white porcelain showed.

We made light conversation waiting for her. It was a pretty town. No, he hadn't lived here all his life. Done thirty years on the police force in the city.

'I wasn't coming here,' he said. 'Not my town, and my wife was gone, two years before. But her father wrote me . . . he wanted to see Andy, and he didn't have anybody to leave the business to. It added up.'

'So, naturally, they made you police chief.'

'Sure. Three hundred a year and some mileage. The force is a traffic cop and a night marshal.'

I said it must be a quiet town.

'It suits me,' Mr. McLane said. 'I guess.'

There was a sort of awkward silence. I broke it by changing the subject. I said, 'Funny name for a woman, Andy.'

Her voice answered me. 'It's Andrea.'

'Not a usual name.'

'Well, I'm used to it.' She was between her father and me, walking to the front door. Fresh lipstick and a hair-combing had not been necessary to make her attractive. She rested her fingertips in the crook of my elbow; the other hand was holding her father's arm, a little more tightly. 'Dad been telling you how green we are in this business?'

'He's been telling me about Mr. Hilliard. We're going to try and sell him a terracer. Maybe some other stuff.'

'John Five? He's got the money for it.'

We were moving up the street together. Sometimes you like people right off. That was the way I felt about these two. They weren't stuffy and they liked each other in a father-and-daughter way that wouldn't have interested Freud for a minute. And, of course, Andy was damned pretty.

The businesspeople of Lowndesburg were coming out of their places, going to lunch. The street was fairly busy. Quite a few people said, 'Hi, Mac,' and about as many greeted Andy. Then Mac said, 'Hello, Ralph,' to a gaunt fellow who didn't answer him.

At once Mac tried to swing back. Andy reached out and caught him firmly by the sleeve. 'Mr. Polette didn't mean to cut you, Dad. He was just preoccupied.'

9

Mac mumbled something about keeping a good deal of money in that fish-face's bank, but he let Andy lead him on. I had revised my estimate of their relationship. It seemed just as warm as ever, but almost a mother-child deal. Mac hadn't looked old enough to be in his second childhood, but I sensed a worry in Andy: a worry, and a wonderful patience.

As we passed the Lowndesburg National Bank, a woman came out and started walking ahead of us.

What is there about a man? I had an extremely nice-looking, nice-talking lady on my arm. I had every chance of getting a date with her tonight, if I stayed over — I'd noticed, no rings; and if I didn't stay over, no Lowndesburg date was going to do me any good.

But here I was, watching the legs of the woman ahead of us with delight, admiring the view of nicely moving hips hugged by a white linen suit. I wanted to see her face . . . I speculated about her age . . . What was it to me? But I looked anyway.

Andy noticed. She said: '*Quelle jambes*, eh, old boy? The shoes cost as much as everything I have on.'

Just then the body on top of the costly white shoes turned left to head for a big Buick station wagon. The bright pleasant day got too hot. The airy, wide street was a choking alley. It was no wonder I'd admired those legs. I'd married them once.

They were the underpinnings of the only person in the world I really hated, my ex-wife. Edith Stayne Porter. Only that wouldn't be her name now. She'd taken me for a lot, but not for the price of Buicks like that station wagon. Apparently Edith had found herself another sucker.

2

Somebody had stopped us and was talking to Mac and Andy about something, I don't know what; and I just stood there and watched that big Buick get driven away by its very expensive driver. There'd been no chance to ask who she was, and I probably wouldn't have anyway. If she hadn't been interrupted, Andy probably would have mentioned the name, small-town fashion.

By the time we had given our order in the Chinese restaurant, I was back in shape again. Mac was asking Andy if she knew whether John Five was in town.

Andy said, 'Henry Lighton and Mrs. John Five were dancing at the hotel last night. They said John Five had gone up to the city to look at a horse or something. He ought to be back late this afternoon . . . Henry's the lawyer for the Hilliard estate, Mr. Porter.'

I said: 'Paul.'

'Well, Paul, then. Are you all right? You look a little green.'

'Oh, I get tired of being the same color all the time.'

I didn't feel like telling an attractive woman that I'd just gotten a shock from seeing my ex-wife. I couldn't talk about Edith without sounding bitter and reproachful, and a woman hearing me could hardly help but wonder what the other side of the story would be. It's a rare marriage that breaks up without there being two sides to the story; I honestly believe ours was the exception.

Mac was saying that he appreciated my staying over, since I couldn't see John Five until late, maybe not till tomorrow. I asked him if there were any other items of our manufacture in the neighborhood, and he said that he hadn't sold any, but maybe the dealer up in the city had, and why didn't I call, and we got into a business discussion.

Andy joined in from time to time — she knew a lot more about the business than she had admitted — and the waitress brought us some very good

13

food. Gradually the nasty feeling I'd gotten from seeing Edith wore off, and I began enjoying myself.

After lunch we went back to the feed-and-seed store, and I phoned the dealer who'd put the terracer in Mac's window. The dealer gave me the names of three farmers around there who'd bought machinery from us, and then he invited me to stay with him and his family if I came through the city. I'd entertained him last time he'd visited the factory, three years ago.

He said, 'Your wife with you, Paul?'

'We're divorced,' I said. 'I'm a bachelor these days.'

While he made the usual awkward remarks, I looked up, and Andy was looking at me. Another woman would have jerked her eyes away; she just smiled.

Later, she got out a county map and showed me where the three customer-farms were, and I asked her if she'd have dinner with me that night.

She said at once, 'I'd love to. We can get a reasonable meal at the hotel, and there's dancing.'

'I'll call for you about seven.'

'Here.' She put a check mark on the map and wrote an address on the margin. 'The mailbox is marked J. F. Gray, for Grandpa, but we live there, too.'

So I checked into the Lowndesburg House, left my baggage, and started out calling on farms.

One of the customers had a land-leveler that dug in at the turns, so I put on my overalls and adjusted the hydraulics for him. That made him offer me a sample of his hobby, which was apple brandy distilled under a special government farmer's permit. I'd never heard of one before, and that led to a second sample and a genial discussion of the high price of liquor; and it was five o'clock when I drove out of his gateway and headed back for Lowndesburg. It was still light, and I drifted along, well pleased with the evening ahead and the day behind me.

About ten past five I was opposite a big arched gateway that said: 'Mr. Hilliard. John Hilliard V, Prop.' It said it in stone relief. Pretty fancy.

15

His lawyer had said he'd be back in late afternoon. I had an hour and three quarters to kill before my date. I turned up the driveway. It wound and climbed through hardwood groves that were not always the native woods. One of the John Hilliards — one to five, take your choice — had been a tree collector. I don't know enough about exotic trees to name them all, but I recognized the flaming red of Chinese pistachios and the fleshy green of Korean camphor-laurel. I passed two men in suntan shirts and green riding breeches, and they were unwrapping a eucalyptus after the winter. So Mr. John Five had his own private forestry service. They were efficient, too; there wasn't a piece of underbrush that didn't look as if it had been placed by an expert.

The private road climbed up on a bluff and stopped; this was Mt. Hilliard. I parked near a six-car garage and looked around. The land fell off sharply ahead of me and behind me. To my right was the garage and the road I'd come up. To my left was a house, or maybe it was a château or a castle. It was huge, I know.

Perversely, all the plantings around it were natives, mostly laurel and myrtle and blue spruce. I followed a path around the house and came out on a half-covered terrace that ran from the front door to the third edge of the bluff. A stone wall kept people from falling down into the common man's valley, but I wasn't there to talk to stone walls.

I pressed a button next to the door, and heard a bell ring deep in the big house and waited. When nothing happened, I rang again. It seemed impossible that a house that big wouldn't have servants; but if they were at the other end, it could take one of them quite a while to get to the front door.

I lighted a cigarette while I waited, and noticed that I'd used the last match in the packet. I made a mental note to get some more packages from the carton in the glove compartment, and put the empty folder back in my pocket. This was not the place to throw litter.

When nobody came, I drifted back to my car. Inside the big garage, I could see the vague outlines of four — no, five cars.

One stall was empty. I started the motor and drove back to town, to my hotel and a bath and a seven o'clock date with Andy McLane.

3

She had on what I guessed was a cocktail suit, silk or a good imitation, pale blue with a black blouse under it. There were earrings shaped like little baskets of fruit, and a pin on the blouse, and so on. Very pleasing.

She said, 'Paul, I'm sorry. Gramps wants us to come have a glass of sherry with him.'

I said I had lived through worse things than that.

'You may be talking before you're fully advised. This way.'

The house was no Mt. Hilliard, but it was bigger than they make them nowadays. There were a lot of plate-glass windows and old-fashioned sliding doors and clear-grained wood paneling, and we walked straight through from the front door to what might have been a back door once; now it led into a conservatory.

It was warmer in there than in the rest

of the house, and considering the age of the man seated bolt upright in an armless straight chair, he could use the heat. He looked as if a couple of 'greats' ought to have preceded his title of Andy's grandfather. The slightest amount of slackness under his jaw indicated that he might once have had a fleshed human body; but all that had gone, years and years ago. Now a skeleton sat erect, covered with gray skin to which large brown freckles failed to give warmth.

Andy said, 'Grandpa, this is — '

He raised a long hand. 'I know. The young man who's taking you out tonight.'

'Paul Porter, Mr. Gray.' This was Otto McLane. I hadn't seen him sitting off to one side, under a scrawny palm that was existing in a mat-covered pot. He held a glass, presumably of sherry; not exactly an ex-cop's drink.

'Give him a glass of wine,' Mr. Gray said. 'Do you drink, young man?'

'Certainly,' I said. 'But seldom sherry.'

Mr. Gray made a noise like *Hmph*, a sound I had previously believed was not a sound at all, but something writers put on paper. 'Give him a glass of sherry, Andrea. Pour yourself one . . . Young man, why are you taking Andrea to dinner?'

'Why do men do anything for women?' I responded. 'Because they think the lady in question is charming, attractive.' I had decided that servility would get me nowhere with him, and anyway, I didn't care very much.

Andy dipped a little curtsey and said, 'Thank you, sir.'

Mr. Gray hmphed around awhile. 'We have plenty of food in the house,' he said. I accepted a glass from Andy and sipped. It wasn't bad; bootless but not repulsive. I waited, and finally the old man said, 'Silly waste of money. Eat here.'

'No, sir,' I said. 'How can I get the gal grateful if I don't spend money on her? And anyway, I'll want a couple of cocktails before my food.'

'Impudent sonofabitch, isn't he, Otto?'

Otto McLane was chuckling. 'He wasn't to me, Mr. Gray. I'd say it was you that brought it out in him.'

'I'll lay off,' J. F. Gray said. He cackled.

'Last amusement of an old man. Sticking pins in young ones to see if they'll wriggle. Hell, I've had two heart attacks and a stroke. Three bowls of pap a day, and a glass of sherry for an old-time whiskey drinker. Call that a life?'

'No. But now that you've given up the act, I'd make a guess you've got some pretty gaudy memories to amuse you over your pap, whatever that is.'

'Super-boiled oatmeal shoved through a sieve,' he said. 'With all kinds of protein and vitamin supplements to make it worse. Hell. Remember a salesman coming in somewhere back in the twenties, trying to get me to sell something like it for hens.' He laughed, or cackled, again. 'I told him it would probably do wonders for the hens, if they could be persuaded to eat it. They couldn't.'

The phone rang. Andy looked at her father, who made a flat down-gesture with the palm of his hand for her to keep her seat, and went himself to snatch up an instrument in the hall. We could hear him easily.

Old Man Gray said, 'So now I'm eating it myself, and I wouldn't be surprised — '

At the same time, Otto McLane was talking on the phone: 'This is Mac . . . Dead? What? All right. I'll go right up there. Give me a couple of minutes start before you tell the state boys. I'd like to be there first.'

The old man had stopped talking when he heard the word 'dead.' He waited, head cocked on one side, and his eyes were as bright as a hen's, and as beady.

Mac stuck his head in, and he no longer looked so much like Harry Truman; his jaw had tightened and pulled all the lines of his face together, so that the benevolence had been replaced with something else, perhaps the cold determination of a cop. He said, 'Police business. Don't wait dinner for me, Mr. Gray.'

'All right, Otto,' J. F. Gray said. 'Give 'em hell, boy.' And Mac was gone.

Andy said, 'Grandpa, if you want us to stay home . . . '

'Hell no. You and Paul go have yourselves a time. I'll slop down my swill and listen to the radio. My eyes can't

23

stand television, Porter.'

'I'll get my hat,' said Andy.

There was an inch or less of sherry left in each of our glasses. The old man raised his. 'To my granddaughter. You married, Porter?'

I grinned. 'What kind of a question is that? No, I'm not.'

'Worried about Andrea. Gave Otto the business so she'd live here with me. It's hard to be old, Porter. Supposed to be a dignified thing to be, but I've never noticed it. Sometimes, in summer, she wears a halter and shorts around the house. You ever noticed the small of a young woman's back?'

'Hell, no.'

'Talking like an old lecher, eh? Not so. Small of the back, right where the spine ends, that's the youngest thing about a young woman. Like to look at it. If I was an old fool, I'd hire a young nurse or a housekeeper, end up marrying her, making an idiot out of myself. Hope I die before Andrea marries and goes away. Don't want to make a fool out of myself.'

'You're quite a guy, Mr. Gray.'

He nodded. His bony hand went out and flicked a leaf off a plant. 'Ought to die. Nothing in life anymore. But nobody ever seems ready to die. Know I'm not. Here's Andrea.'

The hat was made out of a piece of the same stuff the cocktail suit was; it was twisted around and pinned up with a chunk of uncut stone, a pebble set in silver wire.

'Grandpa, you're sure you don't mind?' she asked.

'Otto'll be back. He went off on police business. Maybe he'll tell me about it,' the old man said. 'Can't be much, not in Lowndesburg. A big-city cop like him ought to get it solved in eighteen minutes without breathing hard.'

Andy looked at him hard, frowning. She said, 'Don't be sarcastic,' and then kissed him on the left eyebrow, approximately. I held out my hand, which he waved away as though shaking hands would be too much trouble for him, and we went down the long broad hall towards the front door.

It was dark when we had driven away

from the door light, just the headlamps ahead of us, coming down the highway into town. Andy opened a window and the air was crisp and fresh. 'I like this car, Paul. Yours or the company's?'

'You sound mercenary.'

'Of course. All women look at all young men with an eye to marrying them and being comfortably supported the rest of their lives. And what do all young men think of? Don't tell me, I already know.'

We were coming into the heart of town, the part where the street lamps were. I said, 'You sound like your grandfather.'

A red light and siren came at us fast. I pulled to the sky, and we watched the state car go by. When I started up again, she said something about her grandfather being an old dear, and then we were at the hotel.

We had two cocktails, we had a dance, we had chicken and noodle soup; then we got up to dance again. I was enjoying myself thoroughly, and I think she was. At least, I know she was dancing closer to me than she had at first, a pretty good sign. I tightened my arm around her and looked over at our table, hoping the roast beef wasn't there yet.

It wasn't, but my date's father was. Otto McLane, looking grim and tired and unhappy, was sitting in my chair, his hat in his lap. He caught my eye and raised his chin to call me over.

Not surprisingly, I missed a step and stumbled, and Andy looked up abruptly. I let go of her and took her elbow to guide her to the table; then she saw Mac and made a little noise of distress. 'Something's happened to Grandpa.'

We hurried, almost running, to the table. Mac didn't smile at us. He said, 'I paid your check and canceled the rest of the order. Let's go.'

Andy said, 'Grandpa — '

'Naw. You g'wan home, Andy. Take a cab.'

'Take my car, Andy,' I said. 'You can bring it downtown tomorrow.'

'Take a cab,' Mac said. 'C'mon, Porter.'

It was hard to recognize him as the small-town hay and grain dealer I'd been seeing on and off all day. There was a sour look on his face that might have come from indigestion — the nervous kind, if there is any other.

I said I didn't understand, and I got a look that was almost hatred in return. 'If you want to make a scene here,' he said, 'I got handcuffs, and more than thirty years' experience in putting 'em on. Make something of it, if you want to.'

'Let's go, Andrea,' I said.

Nobody looked at us in the lobby of the hotel; there was nobody on the street at the moment but a couple of cabdrivers, listening to a radio in one of their cars. Mac said again, 'G'wan home, Andy.'

She looked wonderful in the lights from the hotel front; her eyes were hot as St. Elmo's fire. 'Dad, I didn't want to make trouble in there. But I've got a right to know what you're doing. You're acting as if I were twelve years old.'

'It's got nothing to do with you. This is police business. G'wan, scram, now.'

'You're arresting Paul for something?'

Mac said, 'I'm taking him to City Hall for questioning, yeah. And if you want me to say I'm sorry I busted up your date, so okay, it's said.'

'Paul, do you want me to call a lawyer?' she said.

'How do I know? This heavy blanket of mystery's got me covered, too.'

'I'll go this far,' Mac said. 'He needs a lawyer. Henry Lighton's the best in town, Porter, the only good one. You had to be pinched, and I thought it would look better if I came and got you, instead of a uniformed state cop. C'mon.' He shut his mouth and it was obvious there was no hope of getting him to open it. I went along, smiling apologies — what for? — at Andrea.

She ran across the sidewalk and jumped into one of the cabs. I would have watched her drive away, but Mac's hand on my sleeve was strong. 'Did you have an overcoat?'

'It's in my room at the hotel,' I said.

'Suppose you were going to try and get her to go up with you for it later. You got quite a way with the dames, haven't you?'

'Considering Andy's your daughter, you'd know better, if you didn't have a cop's filthy mind. And the rest of the crack hasn't cleared anything up. Some-body file bastardy charges against me?'

McLane said, 'I haven't got a coat on either. No use us freezing.' He jerked my arm and I went along with him.

City Hall was a two-story building set back from the street with trees and a dying lawn around it. A plaque acknowl-edged PWA and WPA help, and through the big front doors I could see the murals that the WPA had once spread through the country.

But we didn't go in the front door; we went around to the side. Here a ramp went up into the Fire Department and stairs went down to the Police Depart-ment. The ramp was marked with a red light and the stairs with a blue. We went down to the blue light.

The police office was nothing: a desk, a phone, two chairs and three filing cases. At the back an open pine door showed a barred one — closed — behind it, leading to the lockup. A triangular sign on the desk said, 'Captain Otto McLane.' Since he was now a chief, that must have been a leftover from his days on the St. Louis force. A captain of municipal police is pretty good; but then I hadn't rated Mac as a dope.

The office was crowded with men. One of them wore the uniform of a state trooper, wide hat and all; the rest of them were quietly dressed, but there was too much muscle under their conservative suits. More state cops, no doubt.

'This is it,' Mac said, and pushed me into the room by the arm he was holding.

I staggered, and bumped into the desk. The uniformed boy steadied me and one of the older men said, 'Take it easy, Chief.'

'Easy, he says,' Mac said. 'It's you I ought to be swinging at. This guy was a guest in my house, he represents one of the solidest companies I do business with, he was out with my daughter, and you guys make me pinch him.'

I said, 'Will somebody tell me what I'm charged with?'

The gray-haired man who'd talked before said, 'Mr. Porter, take it easy. This is very likely to come to nothing.'

'Sure,' Mac said. 'A great big coincidence. I don't believe in them.'

The older man — but he wasn't as old as Mac — said, 'But they happen. Mr. Porter, I'm Lieutenant Detective Gamble, State Police. So we'll know whom we're talking to. You admit you are Paul Porter, of Chicago?'

'If Mac hasn't convinced you of that, I carry a good deal of identification,' I said.

Gamble said, 'Get it out.'

'Very official,' Mac said. 'Big shot — in my town.'

I had my wallet out by then, held it out to Gamble. He said, 'Please take the money out first,' and I did. He thumbed through all the I.D. and credit cards, the driver's license, the insurance cards. Finally he came to the little separate compartment that held my business cards. He looked at these. 'He certainly seems to work for Hydrol Machines, Incorporated, Mac.'

'What detective school did you go to? You can read.'

Gamble said politely — he was the smoothest thing I'd seen in weeks — 'Yes, but printing's cheap. Still, these look good, and since his identity is the only reason for picking him up, let's all act as though he's proved he's Paul Porter.'

'So maybe he bumped off the guy whose I.D. he carries,' Mac said.

Lieutenant Gamble said, 'Mac, no officer likes arresting another cop's friend. Try and get along with us. Mr. Porter, would you mind telling us what you did after lunch today? In as much detail as you can remember, please.'

'Well, after I finished eating,' I said, 'I paid the check, including Mac's lunch — and now you can charge me with bribery.'

The uniformed trooper smiled a little, but Lieutenant Gamble said: 'This is far from being a funny matter, Mr. Porter. On second thought, I think we'll have this taken down and signed by you. If you don't mind.'

'Don't I get a lawyer or something? I'm supposed to be told what I'm accused of.'

Mac jerked a thumb at the cell door behind his office. 'Take a coffee break,

Gamble. Leave him here till be gets a lawyer.'

After Mac's snarl, Gamble's patience and courtesy were monumental. He said: 'Mr. Porter, you've been accused of nothing. But if we're going into talk about lawyers and so on, we can book you, and then you can name your attorney, and then we can wait till we find a magistrate — and so on and so forth. But if you give us a statement, perhaps we can release you at once.'

Mac said: 'Ha!'

Gamble said, 'All right, Chief McLane. But let me point out to you that when you called in the State Police, you ceded authority. I'm in charge of this case at present and will remain so until relieved by a superior.'

'All right.' That was me. 'Let's get it over with. I didn't get to finish my dinner. My name's Paul Porter. I'm vice-president in charge of marketing for Hydrol Machines, Inc., a Chicago firm. Right now I'm engaged on a field trip, visiting users and sellers of our machinery. My boss's name is Harvey Planne, and if you want to check with him, his home phone number is on that card in my wallet.'

The uniformed man, surprisingly, was the stenographer. He had sat down in one of the two chairs, and was writing all this down in his notebook. Perversely, I tried to snow him by talking as fast as I could. I told about the three customers we had here in Lowndes Valley and how I had called on each of them, how long it took, what we talked about. I didn't forget the third one's hobby of making apple brandy, and how we sampled it. The lieutenant seemed to show interest in this. Mac was jumping around like a terrier on a leash.

I hadn't succeeded in snowing the steno at all; he was well up with me when I got to ten past five and the gate at Mt. Hilliard. 'I noticed the time particularly because I naturally didn't want to call on a prospect at a time that might annoy him. It didn't seem too late; I drove up the hill.'

Gamble interrupted me. 'Did anybody see you?'

'I passed two men who looked like foresters or tree surgeons. Whether they noticed me or not, I don't know. Anyway, I got up to the house at whatever time it takes from five-ten to get there, driving reasonably fast on a strange road. I parked and walked around to the front of the building, then rang the bell. When nobody answered, I had a cigarette and waited. It's a big house; might have taken some time to get to the front door. I admired the view, and after a while I went back to my car and drove into town here. It was just about six o'clock when I got my key from the room clerk at the hotel.'

Lieutenant Gamble nodded. Mac was a little quieter; he was watching the lieutenant. Gamble said, 'Now, and this is important, when you got back into your car at Mt. Hilliard, were you still smoking, or did you throw your cigarette away up there?'

So Mt. Hilliard was the important part of the day. I said, 'Let me think . . . I was still smoking. As you come to the gates of Mt. Hilliard, there's a stop sign. I stopped, being a lawful citizen, and before starting up again, I put the butt out in the ashtray of the car.'

'Did you see the two tree surgeons on your way out?'

'Never thought of them. No, I don't think I did.'

Gamble nodded and chewed his lower lip. 'You're willing to sign this?' When I nodded, he turned to the trooper, and said: 'You'll find a typewriter up in the city clerk's office. Type this up — and while you're there, try and get in touch with those men who take care of Mr. Hilliard's trees.'

The trooper said, 'Yes, sir. They're dendrologists, by the way. I asked them once.'

Gamble said that was fine, and the trooper went out. I could hear him clattering up the outside stairs to the ground level.

Gamble continued to chew his lip. Sometimes he would look at Mac and sometimes at me. Finally he said, 'It's an awfully straight story, Mac. You've heard as many as I have in your time. What do you think?'

Mac was more like a well-trained boxer than a terrier now. He said steadily, 'Don't know. If he was lying, he'd have a lot more details. But why ask me? It wasn't my idea to pinch him.'

There was some more silence. Then Gamble sighed and turned to me. 'I can't see what possible harm there can be in telling you what you're up against. John Hilliard got home a little after six, and found his wife dead in the garage. In her car.'

'I thought it must be murder from the way Mac was carrying on. But why me?'

'We didn't even know you'd been up there,' Gamble said. 'You told us that. It makes the case against you just that much worse, and, for some strange reason, makes me begin to believe in your innocence.'

'Why should there be a case against me at all? Just being up there wouldn't be anything — I had a reason; I'd discussed it with McLane here. In fact, it was his idea that I go up there. I never heard of John Hilliard or Mrs. John Hilliard before today, before Otto McLane here mentioned him.'

Lieutenant Gamble said, 'Now you're lying. Now I feel a lot better about this.' He looked at one of his men. 'Take this down. When Trooper Rainier gets back, add this to the statement before Porter signs.' He turned. 'If you'll sign that, too.'

'Of course I will.'

Lieutenant Gamble said slowly: 'Mac, get one of our local J.P.s down to act as magistrate. It's too bad your district attorney's out of town, but we'll take a chance and arraign Porter without a D.A. I wish you had a real jail here, but I'll take Porter up to the city and hold him there as soon as I can.'

'Sure,' said Mac, and he started out.

He didn't make it. An extraordinarily tall, thin man came walking in. I remember thinking his clothes must have cost as much as all the rest of ours put together. He said, 'Evening, Lieutenant, Mac, gentlemen. Mr. Porter, I'm Henry Lighton. Andrea McLane said you might need an attorney.'

'I think I do, sir.'

'Think?'

'I seem to have been near a place where a woman died today. These cops are trying to make it murder, with me the murderer.'

The trooper was back with a sheaf of papers. There seemed to be several copies. Lieutenant Gamble handed them all to the plainclothes man he'd told to take down my statement that I didn't know the Hilliards; he whipped out a fountain pen and wrote rapidly at the end of each copy. Gamble handed them to me.

'Read and sign each one. And please initial the written addendum.'

Henry Lighton smoothed his beautifully graying hair and said, 'Not so fast. I don't think my client's going to sign anything.' He reached out and I handed him a copy.

We both read rapidly; Lighton was humming a little under his breath. 'All of this true, Mr. Porter?'

I said it was.

He said, 'The Hilliard part is obviously the crucial time . . . Oh, sign it. It doesn't mean anything much until it's sworn to.'

When I finished, Henry Lighton said, 'Well, you know where my office is, gentlemen. My client and I are going over there to talk.'

Gamble said, 'I don't think so.'

Lighton asked him if he was in charge of the case.

'I'm in charge, Mr. Lighton, yes,' Gamble said. 'And I think we'll try for an arraignment without bail. You see, that's a false statement, and a false statement in a murder case — '

Henry Lighton held up his hand. 'Please don't tell me the law, Lieutenant. Leave me in my ignorance. Do I tell you how to repair motorcycles?'

'That's a low dig,' said Gamble. 'All right, I'll ask you. When a man says he doesn't know, has never heard of, a woman to whom he was married for four years, would you consider him completely on the up and up?'

I never heard what Mr. Lighton answered to that, because then I couldn't hear at all. There was too much blood in my head; and too many memories, one of them not a day old, of Edith's legs crossing the sidewalk ahead of me and sliding into a big Buick. I tried to say something, but the noise that came out didn't make sense, even to me. Lieutenant Gamble said, 'Get him a glass of water.'

I heard that, and I felt hands lowering me into a chair, and then the water was at my lips. I swallowed with difficulty, but it helped me. I said, 'Edith? I saw her in town today.' My head wasn't throbbing so badly. 'McLane was with me. On our way to lunch.'

Mac said, 'Yeah, I was. I remember.'

'Ah, yes,' said Henry Lighton, 'you'd remember, all right. She could make a man's day — '

'Why didn't you tell me she was Mrs. Hilliard?'

Mac turned to me. 'Why didn't you tell me she was your wife?' There was a querulous, little-boy note in his voice. 'We found it out when we talked to John Five. Asked him about enemies. He said maybe her ex-husband, Paul Porter. Then the two tree surgeon guys said an Illinois car

42

had been up there but didn't stay long.'

'I think a mistake's been made,' Lieutenant Gamble said. 'I think I'm going to turn you loose. When you heard your wife — your ex-wife — was dead, you weren't faking that reaction. Let me tell you, most killers and many other felons are psychopaths. Where other people react sharply, they react by getting calmer. I took you for one of them.'

McLane was changing back into the small-town businessman. Having been a boxer and a terrier, he now began to resemble a basset — a whole kennel of dogs in one man. I hoped I'd be able to see him again someday without thinking of canines; I doubted it. He said, 'See how it looked to me. A guy comes in and says he's with the company that makes a rig I got in my window. I don't ask him for credentials; why should I? He buys me a cheap lunch and steers the talk around to where I give him — me, the chief of police — a reason to go to a woman's house where he wants to kill, maybe has good reason to kill — the woman. I even tell him that she'll be alone there, 'cause

43

her husband'll be out; and it's Thursday, when even a cop knows rich people's servants get off.'

I said, 'I didn't know that. I didn't know Mrs. Hilliard was — who she was.'

'But see how it looked to me,' Mac said. 'It looked like a guy'd deliberately set out to use me for a patsy. Me, who'd been a captain of detectives in one of the ten largest cities in the United States.' There was a wail in his voice that was hard to explain. 'Gone out of his way to make a sucker of me!'

Henry Lighton said, 'Now, Mac, take it easy. There's life in the old dog yet.'

Considering my kennel-reflections, this startled me, and I grinned at Lighton. He remained grave. But he had explained what was wrong with the chief: Mac was afraid he was all washed up, too old to be of any use in the world. Considering the age of the father-in-law he lived with, he should have thought of himself as a pup, with many years ahead in which to be a gay dog. Apparently he didn't. He hadn't been trying to clear me because he loved me, but because he didn't. He was afraid that the cops were regarding him as useless, were laughing at him.

'Believe me, Mr. McLane,' I said, 'I'd never heard of you before today. And I didn't know Edith had remarried.' This time I said the name without difficulty.

Lieutenant Gamble said, 'Mind telling us the circumstances of your divorce?'

'You're damned well right I do!'

'Take it easy, client,' Henry Lighton said. 'You don't swear at police officers any more than you call them cops.'

'Or motorcycle repairmen,' Gamble said.

This got a smile from Henry Lighton. It was as aristocratic as the rest of him. He made the dingy office look dingier when he smiled. He said, 'I think that all the lieutenant wants to know is whether you went to court, defaulted . . . the legal circumstances of the case.'

Gamble said, 'I wanted a good deal more than that, but if Mr. Lighton says that's all you're going to give me, I'll settle for it.'

We were all very polite with each other. Henry Lighton bowed to the lieutenant

45

and gestured to me, and I said: 'We'd been separated a year, eleven months to be exact, when I got a letter from a Nevada lawyer. He enclosed a copy of the divorce decree, and advised me to hang on to it if I wanted to remarry. I haven't. I — '

'That's enough,' Henry Lighton said. 'May we go now, Lieutenant?'

Gamble said, 'I'd like your client to see me before he leaves town. I understand he's paid for a room till morning; maybe by then I'll know more about the case.' He paused. 'Mr. Porter, whether it damages your feelings or not, by morning I'll want to know more about the deceased's background.'

I nodded. Henry Lighton took my arm, and we started out. McLane suddenly came to life. 'Wait a minute. I noticed something today: you don't carry a cigarette lighter.' He was very proud of himself; you could hear it in his voice. 'A thing I've noticed, since I've been in business. Salesmen all carry matches with their company name on them. You say you smoked a cigarette up at John Five's;

46

you put it out down at the stop sign. How about the match?'

Lieutenant Gamble was getting impatient, but I could see Mac's point. If the tree surgeons saw me come down the mountain, they'd say I'd just had time to smoke one cigarette, and a man wouldn't hold a smoke while killing a woman. I said, 'This is going to look so pat it's suspicious. I threw the match away right at the front door of the house, mansion, whatever you call it. It hasn't rained since then, so maybe you can find it. And here's the book it came from. It was the last in the book, and Mt. Hilliard looked too neat to litter up.'

I fished the book out and threw it on the desk. 'I was never a big-city police captain, like our friend McLane here, but I imagine anybody with a magnifying glass can tell if a match was torn from this pack or another. You're not going to accuse me of murdering with one hand and holding a cigarette with the other, are you?'

'If the match is there — and somehow or other I'm sure it will be — it'll either

47

fit the tear or not. It's impossible, without machinery, to tear two matches exactly alike.'

Mac growled something I couldn't get, but Lieutenant Gamble said: 'Yes, Mac. It does look pat, as though he'd planted the match to account for his time up there.'

Mac said, 'Sure. Who carries empty matchbooks in his pocket?'

'I do,' I said. 'If you're going to sell expensive machinery to a man, you don't start out by dirtying up his front lawn with a piece of advertising.'

Henry Lighton said, 'Mr. Porter, please stop bickering with these officers. You have me to do that for you.'

'This sews it all up,' Mac said. 'Honest men don't set up alibis for themselves. He expected to get pinched when he threw that match away, and that's why he kept the match folder!'

Lieutenant Gamble said, 'Oh, Chief,' in a weary voice.

'He wanted to account for his time,' Mac barked. 'Honest men don't care about that.'

This time Lighton took it. 'Oh, Mac, take it easy.'

A state trooper I hadn't seen before came in, saluted Gamble, and said: 'Sir, I made a pickup on those tree men. They were at a movie in town.'

Henry Lighton laughed. 'Who's being pat now? We talk about tree surgeons giving Mr. Porter an alibi — and tree surgeons show up.'

McLane said, 'That kind of coincidence can happen, sure. But — '

Lieutenant Gamble waved a tired hand. 'Gentlemen, we're talking ourselves to death. Would you ask the dendrologists to step in, Trooper?'

The word startled the trooper so that he forgot to salute. He opened the door and said, 'In here, please.'

Two big guys came in, and a woman. Lieutenant Gamble said, 'I didn't send for the lady, Trooper.'

The state trooper said, 'Lieutenant, I don't know what a dend — what you said is.'

Henry Lighton made a contribution. 'At any moment the chorus will dance in, singing something appropriate from Gilbert and Sullivan.'

The big guys looked alike, though they no longer wore John Five's uniforms. One of them said, 'Dendrology is the study of trees. A dendrologist is — '

'All right,' Lieutenant Gamble said. 'I didn't invite you here for a lecture on English. What are your names?'

I know the one on the left,' McLane said suddenly. 'He goes out with my daughter. He calls himself Daniel Banion.'

'Well, it's my name,' the one on the left said. 'This is my partner Harold Crosley. The lady is his wife. And what's this all about, Mr. McLane?'

Mac said: 'The lieutenant is in charge.'

'Well, that's right,' Lieutenant Gamble said. 'You two men saw Mr. Porter here drive up to Mt. Hilliard this afternoon. Right?'

Banion said, 'We saw a car with an Illinois license drive up. I didn't see the driver, to recognize.'

'How about you, Crosley?'

'We were talking about the red spiders

50

that have gotten in the Pfitzers up there,' Crosley said. 'We were pretty absorbed.'

Gamble said, 'If anybody wants to know what Pfitzers are, or what red spiders do in them, please wait till you get outside. Did you see this Illinois car come down off the hill again?'

'No,' said Crosley.

Lieutenant Gamble said, 'The first short answer all evening, thank the Lord.' He turned to Henry Lighton. 'The whole thing about the match doesn't signify anything now, does it, counselor?'

Henry Lighton smiled his urbane smile and said: 'Mr. Crosley, did you or your associate *hear* the car come down? And Pfitzers are a variety of low-growing juniper, Lieutenant.'

Lieutenant Gamble said: 'God.'

Banion said, 'Why, yeah, we heard a car come down, about fifteen minutes after Mr. Porter went up.'

'As John Five's lawyer,' said Henry Lighton, 'I'm familiar with Mt. Hilliard. No way for a car to come down without seeing this Illinois tagged automobile — which might have been anybody's from

Illinois, Lieutenant — parked up there, would there be, Mr. Crosley, Mr. Banion?'

Banion said: 'Nope.'

Henry Lighton said, 'Client, let's go to my office for a chat.'

'God help the district attorney when he comes up against you, Mr. Lighton,' Gamble said. 'My men are up there searching, and if the match is there they'll find it. I suppose if it doesn't fit the book, or if they don't find it, you'll accuse me of tampering with the evidence.'

'I wouldn't think of it,' Henry Lighton said. 'And don't use the name of the Deity so often, Lieutenant. It becomes banal, after a while.' We walked out.

4

It was colder than when Mac had taken me into City Hall. I shivered. Henry Lighton looked at me and said, 'Is your overcoat back there?'

'In my hotel room. I wasn't going to be out except in a heated car.'

There were quite a number of people around the Hall now; they were watching the front door. Then they saw us and hurried over. One of the men said, 'That must be the murderer now.'

Lighton had hold of my arm again and was hurrying me across the crisp frost-killed grass. 'Don't say anything, Porter. Act as if they aren't there.'

A fat woman said: 'They wouldn't be letting him go if he was guilty.'

A man said: 'If he wasn't guilty, what'd he hire Henry Lighton for?'

The hand on my arm tightened, and Henry Lighton chuckled. 'Such is fame.'

The people tried to stop us but Henry

Lighton glared them out of the way. They were much more polite than a city crowd. They didn't actually block us; they were just slow in giving way.

Then a kid, not more than eighteen or nineteen, said, 'I'm from the *Lowndesburg Journal*, and the A.P. I'd like to know — '

Lighton said, 'No comment, Max. I'll call your dad if we have a statement later.'

The kid looked crushed, and we went on. Henry opened the plate-glass door of what looked like a remodeled Colonial dwelling. 'They're either too young or too old,' he said.

I looked surprised. He went on: 'My office is upstairs here. Weren't you thinking that, over in the police office? Mac's worried that you picked his town to commit a murder in because he's too old to be a serious menace to a murderer. Makes no sense at all, but you know, people seldom do make sense.'

We were at the top of the curving staircase now. What must have originally been bedrooms were now offices, each with a different name on the door. Mr.

Lighton had no partners listed, but maybe the whole building belonged to one firm.

He opened the door and bowed me in. 'Here's your boy, Andy.'

She got up from a deep leather chair. The place was furnished like an Englishman's club in a movie — heavy desk, high-backed swivel chair in a bay window, and all the rest, deep carpet and leather furniture and hunting prints on the wall — and the result was to make Andy McLane look fragile and thoroughly feminine and very desirable. Well, she'd looked desirable before, but not the other things.

Henry Lighton went behind the desk and sank down in the swivel chair. 'I can turn,' he said, 'and the City Hall, with all its entrances and exits, is spread before me like a panoply of virtue and vice.' He turned and was hidden from us by the high back of his chair.

Andy held out both hands to me. 'I'm sorry our date was ruined,' she said. 'I was having a good time.' She smiled and got her fingers back from me. 'By the way, I called Grandpa. He said he'd pay Henry Lighton's fee. He must have taken quite a liking to you.'

'Maybe he thinks you like me. He's pretty crazy about you.'

She let me make what I wanted out of a smile.

I said, 'For what it's worth, I didn't kill her. Or anybody. And you knew I was divorced.'

Andy said, 'That's hardly my business. And it really isn't my business, either, how Grandpa spends his money. A man his age is entitled to his — his — '

''Eccentricities' is the word you want,' I said. 'Do you consider it eccentric to like me?'

She let me have another smile on that.

Henry Lighton turned. 'Since you aren't going to neck,' he said, 'there's no use my being delicate.'

Andy said: 'Blush, blush.'

'We've got a long night ahead of us,' Henry Lighton said. 'I have to get to know my client, inside out, right side back again, upside down. Andy, darling, if you aren't afraid of going out into the night, how about cruising down to Larry Genauer's emporium of good cheer and getting (a) a bottle of Scotch, (b) two large bottles of soda, and (e) a sack of ice cubes? Put it on my bill and I'll charge it to Mr. Gray.'

'Mr. Gray doesn't have to pay your fee. I'll be glad to.'

'Take blessings as they fall, Paul, if I may call you Paul. On your way, Andy.'

When she was gone, Henry Lighton said: 'It's going to hurt you, kid, but I have to know. Did you have any reason for killing Edith Hilliard?'

I sat down in the chair nearest the desk. The room was lighted by a brass Federalist lamp on the desk. I stared at it and said: 'Yes.'

Henry Lighton said, 'Want to wait till you've oiled your tongue a little? It's why I sent for the Scotch.' Without waiting for me to answer, he went on, 'You ought to know a little more about me. Several years ago I was one of the best criminal lawyers in New York. My income ran into six figures, which is no hay, especially when it comes to paying the income tax.

But I saw no sense in all that and came out here and bought a farm out in the valley. You passed it today, right next to that of our apple-brandy-loving friend, Jack Lutyel. Farming bored me, so I rented this office. I do a little law work, but I'm no hick, friend, and you are damned lucky I'm not. You're in trouble.'

'Seemed to me when they let me go, they meant it.'

'Mac's like a bulldog. Why do people always think of dogs when they talk about Otto McLane? I guess it's his sad eyes.'

'No one can say a word against McLane. He was the one who brought up the match, and tried to clear me.'

'Just to prove he was smarter than Gamble . . . and, then, for the same reason, he proved the match meant nothing. But Mac doesn't matter. The trouble you're in is big. It's an awful coincidence that an ex-husband would drift into town just on the day a woman gets killed. An ex-husband with rancor, if I'm right.'

'You're right.'

'She didn't send for you? If she was

going to take you back, it would give John Hilliard Five a motive that would fix him. If she sent for you, now's the time to tell me.'

'She didn't send for me. I didn't know where she was, didn't know she'd remarried.'

He cleared his throat, made a steeple out of his fingers, and leaned back in his regal chair. He stared at the ceiling. 'Oh, brother. You must live right, as the kids say. If you'd gotten here tomorrow, or any other day in the long history of Lowndesburg, you'd have been all right.'

'Tell me about McLane and his father-in-law,' I said. 'It's really weird that the old man would hire me a lawyer on the strength of five minutes and a glass of sherry.'

Henry Lighton shrugged. 'Maybe Andy told him she'd fallen in love with you on first sight . . . But I don't think so. I think he doesn't like Mac; and when he thought Mac arrested you, he decided to take a hand, show Mac up for a fool.'

'But he gave Mac the business.'

Henry Lighton began chuckling. It was

a very musical sound. 'In more ways than one. The old man wanted Andrea around. Mac's the price of that. Call them two superannuated dogs, fighting over a manger.'

'There you go comparing Mac to a dog again. And Andy's the manger?'

He said, 'We're way off the point. Did you kill Edith Hilliard?'

'I didn't know she was here. I didn't see her.'

'You're getting shrill. Watch that. Juries send people to the chair not because they're guilty, but because they don't like them, and being shrill is an easy way to be disliked.'

I said, 'Damn it, Mr. Lighton, I — '

The outer door opened, and Andrea McLane was back. She had turned the big collar of her tweed coat up, and it framed her head; her hair was glistening. 'It's beginning to rain out.'

Henry Lighton turned in his big chair and looked out at the City Hall and its lawn and its sycamores. 'So it is,' he said. 'And some more cops have arrived. Big brass, from the size of their cars. It's a curious thing. The lowest grade of policeman, the patrolman, has to get to what the newspapers call the scene of the crime fastest, so they give him the cheapest, slowest car. The very top grade of policeman can take his time, so he gets the fastest car. Well, I guess it makes as much sense as anything in this . . . '

He went on. But I had long since given up listening to him. I was staring at Andy as though I'd never seen a woman before. The color the cold had brought to her cheeks, the shine that the rain had given to her hair, made her seem finally, and without doubt, the most desirable thing I'd ever seen.

So this is how it comes to you. After a marriage, after a half dozen more or less comfortable love affairs, this is how it hits. It isn't a completely pleasant sensation, I learned; nor have the better poets ever claimed it was.

She went by me and put her two paper bags down on Henry Lighton's desk. He was still talking; something about the over-complications of a totally mechanical civilization. Her packages unloaded, she turned back to me. Slowly her hands came up and were held out to me — a curious gesture, because the arms must have come up with them, since I knew that only the hands were for me.

I grabbed them both, and pressed them in my own palms. Her hands were very cold, but their touch melted the ice in my belly, and I was self-confident again.

The slight creak of Henry Lighton's swivel chair brought us back to earth. He said, 'Well, it's time for me to make hostly gestures and noises. You'll have a drink with us before you go, Andy?'

She jumped a little. 'Yes. Of course.'

Henry Lighton moved around the office, getting glasses from a hard-pine cupboard, opening bottles, fishing ice up with his long fingers. He handed a glass to Andy, one to me. 'Here's to litigation, the lawyer's life blood.'

Andy said, 'You're damned funny, Henry.'

'The light touch,' Henry Lighton said. 'Convinces the jury that you're sure of getting your client off. Or sometimes it does.'

Andy said, 'I'm dying of laughter. Every time you mention the jury, I choke with glee. Didn't you ever try and stop an injustice before it got to a jury?'

'End of humor,' he said. 'Appearance of serious-minded attorney. Paul hasn't a chance of not going to trial, unless they catch the murderer or frame one. The circumstances are too damned weird.' He stopped, then added, 'None of this is any of your business, Andy. I don't want to talk about it till I figure out a defense.'

I had only drunk half my highball. Now I set it down on the edge of the desk so hard that the liquor jumped and spilled on the wood, where it fizzed shallowly. 'Damn it, I didn't kill her. And before I got through over at the police station, they didn't think I had, or they wouldn't have let me go. Whose side are you on, anyway?'

'Yours,' Henry Lighton said. 'And they didn't exactly let you go. There's no district attorney available for this county tonight. With me on your side, they were afraid of arraigning you illegally, so I could throw the arraignment out later, and I would have seen it was done that way. But they didn't let you go. Try getting out of Lowndesburg! They know where you are: in my office. They impounded your car a long time ago; try getting another one. Try going anyplace except to the hotel from here, and then try getting out of the hotel.'

I told him I saw his point.

Lighton said, 'Well, don't let it crush you. I'm a good lawyer, and I'm not as damned frivolous as I sound. As soon as Andy's out of the way, we'll start on the story of your marriage, and somehow or other I'll start building up a case.' He smiled. 'There's another room, Andy. Take your drink with you.'

She smiled at me and went into what I guess was the secretary's office, and I was alone with my lawyer.

'Andy didn't have to go,' I said. 'It's a quick story. I had some money; some saved, some inherited. She told me she was pregnant to get me to marry her, and then she told me it was a mistake, and then she ran through my money and then she ran out. Period.'

'She had the most beautiful legs I've ever seen, and a face that made you dream of a woman without guile, malice or greed. It almost surprised you that she had to eat, like other mortals.'

I must have looked almost as amazed as I felt.

'All right,' Lighton said. 'I had a case for her, a yen, a crush on her, whatever the current vulgarism is. Where did John Five meet her, do you know?'

'I already told you I didn't know she'd remarried. The divorce papers came from Reno.'

'John Five was west — California, Las Vegas, San Francisco — for a while. I paid his bills for him while he was away.'

'She liked money,' I said. 'She'd go where it was.'

'We all like money.' He got up and refilled his glass, gesturing to me. I shook my head. I had the feeling I'd stepped into a new world where everyone's objective was to trap me. I would be a fool to trust anyone in Lowndesburg. The time to get drunk was not now.

The phone rang. Henry Lighton raised

his thin eyebrows at it, and then lowered them and picked up the phone. He said his name. 'No, I'm not . . . not yet . . . I don't see that that matters . . . No, I couldn't. But before you ask anyone else, I'd like you to come to my office, now to meet him. You might change your mind . . . Well, do that.'

He hung up and smiled. 'John Five. Wanted to retain me as special prosecutor. I told him to come up here and talk to you. He said he'd think it over.'

'I don't see what's to be gained by — '

'Don't be a child,' said Lighton. 'John Five laid the original finger on you. If he takes it off, it would help.'

'Is he likely to because I'm pretty, or wear a nice blue suit?'

'The only picture of you that he's had was from Edith,' Henry Lighton said. 'She may have made you out as a monster of some kind. Meeting you can't help but be to our advantage. He might come here. He just might. Men are curious about their wives' ex-husbands. That's enough for now.' He pressed a button, and a buzzer sounded next door.

'You're the most peculiar lawyer I've ever seen,' I said. 'You don't seem to plan at all. You just let things happen.'

Andy came back in, with another smile for me.

'They happen whether we let them or not, don't they?' my attorney said. He stood up and started walking around the room. After a while he started talking local politics to Andy. She answered him, and I lost interest in a conversation that was all about people I didn't know.

I got up and fixed myself another highball. 'Perhaps I ought to call my boss, Harvey Planne. Our lawyers would know somebody down here to represent me, or maybe one of them could come down himself.' I reached in my hip pocket to get Harvey's home phone number, and then I remembered Lieutenant Gamble had kept the wallet. He'd be checking everybody in it to find out about me. And that wasn't good. I had no more to hide than the next man, but it is not very good for a businessman to have police around asking questions about him.

I hadn't been with Harvey Planne and Hydrol very long. Why should he send legal help or any kind of help?

And I didn't have much money. I was barely back on my feet again after the wreck Edith had made of my bank account and my career. A divorce never leaves you exactly as it found you, I suppose.

Perhaps a third highball would help . . . Before, getting drunk had seemed a very bad idea, the worst in the world; a man in a trap should keep his wits steady. But now that it was reaching me that, outside the trap, I didn't have a friend in the world — not a real friend — drinking seemed the dandiest of ideas, and I'm not a heavy drinker.

Andy and Henry Lighton were talking about some people named Madge and Jimmy, who seemed to be local politicians, or as reasonable a facsimile of same as Lowndesburg could be expected to produce. Madge, it seemed, was for Jimmy, but susceptible to flattery, and might desert him at any moment. 'Fond as she is of Jimmy, she'd always go for three men against one,' Andy said.

Henry Lighton said, 'But if we had one voice there, to put our side forward, it would get on the record.' He turned to me. 'What are you up to?'

'I'm going over to the hotel.'

'No. I'm not through with you yet.'

'But, I should think, the client — '

His voice turned very harsh. 'My clients do what I tell them. You stay.'

'The law isn't a license that gives you the right to play with people like — '

He cut me off. I didn't know what I was going to say anyway.

'Liberty,' he said. 'Not license. I can play around with people because I get them off in court. Look up my record some time. Come in tomorrow — if I decide you're still loose then — and my secretary will get it out for you. People are so frightened I won't defend them that they gladly surrender their lives, their fates, their very wives to me — if I want them to.'

Andy said, 'Really, Henry.'

He flung himself around his desk and fell into his high-backed chair. 'Just histrionics,' he said. 'All criminal lawyers are hams. Just showing off. Did I dominate you, Porter?' I didn't answer. I hated him thoroughly just then.

'That was a sample of what I would have been if I'd stayed in big-time practice. So . . . I got out. Just about in time, too.'

A siren wailed down in the square. It sounded like a loon I'd heard once, in a camp in Maine. I had fallen among loons, I felt, but not the bird kind.

Another one appeared then, as though conjured out of the air by my thoughts. It was McLane, Otto McLane. He had on a blue uniform, with an eagle on each shoulder, like an army colonel's eagle, but in brass.

He put his hands on his blue serge hips and said, 'What the hell are you doing here?' to his daughter.

'Sitting and talking to Mr. Lighton and Mr. Porter.'

'I went home to get my uniform,' he said, 'so Gamble wouldn't have to keep explaining me to the brass, and you weren't there. I didn't raise you to hang out with murderers and shysters. G'wan home.'

'Dad, leave me alone,' she said.

Henry Lighton said, 'You know, Chief, this is my office. You ought to say something like 'permission to come aboard,' or 'thanks for the use of the hall,' before you call me a shyster. You really should, Chief.' His use of the word 'chief' was a masterpiece of understated insult.

Mac glared at him and walked across to me. 'Leave my daughter alone, punk.'

I said, 'Mac, before we start anything else, thanks for the help you gave me over there.'

'I don't frame innocent guys. And I don't let state brass, no matter how big, crowd me out of my own department. But that's nothing to you. I don't want a guy who's suspected of murder chasing after my daughter. Get it, punk?'

I understood him. A washed-up man still trying to be impressive. But I'd been pushed too far. I'd had it. 'Chief McLane,' I said, 'I'm not a known pickpocket that you can tell to get out of your one-horse town. Float, isn't that the word that cops use? You can't float me.'

'Big shot,' Mac said. 'Chicago big shot.'

'Has-been,' I said. 'Lowndesburg has-been. From now on, if you talk to me, do it through my lawyer here, or Lieutenant Gamble.'

Dogs don't turn whitish-green with rage, so Mac longer looked canine. He said, 'Gamble! I was a police officer when Gamble needed changing on the hour!'

'And he's a police officer when you're part-time day watchman in a feed store!'

Henry Lighton said, 'Your relationship with the police department deteriorates rapidly. Hold it, Chief.'

I turned and looked at Mac. He was getting out a gun from under the blue skirt of his tunic. 'You and me, punk, are going for a walk. When I bring you back, you'll be willing to talk! You're going to tell me how, when, why and dot your i's and cross your t's, and then we'll see your great pal Gamble, and — '

'I said, Chief, hold on,' Lighton said.

We both looked over at the desk. He was pointing a small efficient-looking automatic at Mac. 'I'm sorry, Mac. I like your father-in-law, I'm mad about your daughter, and I used to like you. But the dignity of the bar is not to be trod on lightly, like the snake in the old Revolutionary flag.'

Mac called him one of the more obvious epithets.

'I must also warn you that a tape recorder has been running since you first insulted my client. Don't add any more to it.'

McLane turned on his heel and slammed out. The building was well made, or it would have shaken from the banging he gave the door.

'What an unrewarding conference. Oh, for God's sake,' said Henry Lighton.

Andrea McLane had burst into tears.

I must have hurried over to her, because I found myself standing in front of her, holding out my arms, trying to take her in them. But she side-stepped, smiled a wan smile that wasn't more than kindly and friendly, and reached up and patted my cheek.

Suddenly I realized that I'd been living in a fantasy, a dream world where Andy

McLane loved me. But all that was between us was a couple of dances, a bowl of noodle soup, and two cocktails. Well, she'd held my hand a couple of times, which is hardly a passionate affair for a modern woman.

She had cried, and maybe it was for me and maybe it was because her father had just shown himself a jerk and a washout. Reason enough to be sad, especially when I remembered how protective she'd been towards him that morning.

Lighton said, 'Now you know why Mr. Gray was willing to pay your bill here. All of Mac's friends are afraid he's blown his stack. Oh, call it . . . call it the male change of life.' He stopped and considered this, and his eyes brightened with admiration for his own words. When he spoke again, he didn't sound so angry. 'Andy, I'll let you take Mr. Porter to his hotel where you can kiss him good night. I'll pick you up at the lobby entrance in ten minutes and drive you home where you can — hope springs eternal — kiss *me* good night. Don't cry; think of all the joys ahead of you.'

5

The lobby of the hotel had, the few times I'd seen it, been a sleepy place with a drowsing clerk, a Coke machine, and the entrance to the night club/restaurant. Outside of the lights necessary for these, there were dark corners and overstuffed leather chairs, a few of them oozing their overstuffing.

New life had come into the old place. At least two dozen men and a couple of women were milling around, and the management had honored them with a lighted chandelier that looked about to fall from the weight of dust on its mass of tortured glass and metal. Three of the men and one of the women were talking to a uniformed state police lieutenant over in one corner, near the Coke machine. I wouldn't say they had cornered him; he looked expansively happy, waving beefy hands and beaming.

Andy said: 'I don't get my good-night kiss.'

'I like the way you put that. I like it very much. Not so much as I would have liked kissing you.' I thought, *There's always my room.*

'In front of God and the Associated Press? No thanks.'

'There'll be another — ' But the press had seen us. They deserted the lieutenant, who went on waving his hands and talking for a good three seconds before he saw he'd lost his audience. Then they were on me, and Andy fled out of the front door and away.

A lady reporter asked me, 'You're Mr. Porter, I just know it, and I want to know, do you have a picture of your wife?'

'My ex-wife. And I don't carry ex-wives' pictures near to my heart.'

A thin, bald gent with his hat tilted back to show that grass didn't grow on his busy street said, 'How many times you been married, Porter?'

'Just the once.'

He put the hand that held his notepaper on one hip, the one holding his pencil on the other, and shot his head out at me. He had a remarkably long neck. 'You said ex-wives, not ex-wife.'

A fat reporter came to his aid. 'It's better not to hold out on the press, Mr. Porter. If you've been married before, we'll find it out.'

The imaginary headlines swam before my eyes: POLICE BACKTRACK BLUE-BEARD. Or words to that effect. 'No previous marriages,' I said. 'I guess I was making a little joke.'

At once they all made notes on the folded coarse paper they carried. ALLEGED SLAYER QUIPS. Maybe I should have been a headline writer.

The previously silent lady reporter edged up to me. She had a less piercing voice than her colleague, but was otherwise equally a reject. 'You're very attractive, you know, Mr. Porter. I'll just bet you've got a new girlfriend.'

'No such luck,' I said, to be saying something.

Fat man said, 'Wasn't that a woman that just came in with you?'

'The police chief's daughter,' I said. At

once I knew I shouldn't have, and tried to recover lost ground. 'Maybe the cops are short-handed, and swore her in. Anyway, she drove me back from across the square.' It wasn't a very good recovery. Bluebeard was quipping again.

They all turned, and pushed a young kid out of the crowd. It had been dark out on the courthouse lawn, but I thought he was the one who had tried to interview Henry Lighton and me, the one Henry had called Max. They were either too young or too old, the lawyer had said.

The rest of the mob started asking him if the woman who'd brought me to the hotel really was the police chief's daughter. They asked him so energetically that he didn't have a chance to answer for a while. When he did, he sounded miserable. 'I didn't see her. But Chief McLane's daughter is tall and dark and she's not a woman. She's older, about twenty-seven or -eight.'

Although this didn't seem to go over so well with the two lady reporters, it did provide a diverting action to save me. The ladies just glared at poor young Max, and the thin reporter, who seemed to be a leader of some sort, chuckled, and then they were down my throat again.

One of the men in the back shouted, 'You been released, Porter?'

'Yes.'

'Going back to Chicago tonight?'

'I've been told not to leave town.'

This made them all very happy. They made little notes again. All but young Max, who was trying to edge away. Henry Lighton had said it was Max's father's paper; I didn't think the son was going to follow in the paternal footsteps.

The thin man shot his head out again. 'Have there been any other arrests?'

I said I didn't know.

'Then you're still the only suspect?'

'I don't know that, either. All know is, I was told I could get some sleep, and I'd very much like to.'

Fat man took over. 'What you so tired for? Just an ordinary day, wasn't it? Called on a few customers, took it easy, didn't you?'

'Ending up with being arrested, held, questioned. I'm not accustomed to that kind of night work.'

A voice from the back said: 'He's bluffing. I've seen a lot of murderers, and the cool ones are always bluffing. An innocent guy, now, he'd be in tears.'

Even as my temper left me, I knew I was making a mistake. Alienating the press, it's called, I think. But I'd had all I could stand. I said: 'That's probably slander. And if you want anything else, go see my attorney, Henry Lighton. In the meantime — ' I raised my voice. 'Lieutenant!'

He was out there beyond the crowd of reporters, looking lonely. He turned, and brightened; we all need to be needed. 'Yes, sir?'

'I could use a little police protection. I want to get to my room, and I don't see how I can through this mob.'

He waded over. He was a very different type from Lieutenant Gamble; fat where the plainclothes officer was muscular, dull-eyed where Lieutenant Gamble was sharp and alert-looking. I guess it takes different types to do different kinds of police work; I don't know. I never wanted to see another policeman again in this or any other life.

'Break it up, folks,' he said. 'The poor guy is probably tired, and anyway, anything he's got to say, he oughta be saying it to the authorities.'

But it did the work for me; they turned on him just long enough to let me slip by. They were asking him if he'd say I was being held incommunicado just as I made it to the stairs. The elevator was on the ground floor, but I thought I could do better on my own legs.

When I opened the door of my room, the phone was ringing. I snatched it up, and the operator said I hadn't stopped at the desk for my messages. When I confessed to this heinous crime, she said she had a call for me from Chicago; she'd ring me back if I would promise to stay in my room. I promised.

I used cold water on my face and tried to think a cheerful thought, and finally the phone rang again. The hotel operator said: 'Your call from Chicago, Mr. Porter.'

There was no hope she wouldn't listen in. How often does a town with a three-hundred-a-year police chief have a murder?

The call was from Harvey Planne. He said: 'What are you doing in Lowndesburg? Where the hell is Lowndesburg, and what the hell are you doing there? Police types have been all over me all evening.'

Harvey was a lend-lease officer with the British in '42 and '43, and he never lost his British accent. If he had, he would have gone back and looked for it.

I told him it was rather complicated, and then I went into details. Despite my warning, I didn't feel he was getting the story at all.

When I finished, he said, 'Bit sticky, isn't it? I mean time-consuming, to say the least. Tell you what. I'll send you a month's pay, first thing in the Ack Emma, and you consider yourself on indefinite leave of absence. Don't worry; your job will be here when, as and if.'

When I cleared myself, as long as no shadow rested on me and therefore on the firm, and if his father didn't object. Harvey was founder and president of

Hydrol, but his father was chairman and sole investor.

But I might need the job back, so I thanked him as though he'd done me a big favor, and left him, I hope, thinking he had. I was now on my own. I couldn't think of another friend that the divorce had left me. Then I was alone in that damned hotel room, a picture of some-place in spring on the wall, and a hole in the door through which you could send clothes, and a bed and a closet and a chair. The drinks Henry Lighton had given me churned in my stomach and died an unhappy and protesting death, and I felt like I'd like to die with them.

This morning — my God, just the same day, for it wasn't midnight yet — I had driven into Lowndesburg. Good job, good car, good weather. The chances of my driving out of Lowndesburg again, at the wheel, un-handcuffed, were not quite up to those of a Percheron winning the Kentucky Derby. I was cooked, but good. I had a sadistic cynic for a lawyer, no friends, and a damned good case against me.

The phone rang. I stared at it — it was probably the FBI joining the case, with a complete set of my fingerprints found on a long-handled stiletto — and it rang again and again. I picked it up. Henry Lighton said, 'Paul, I want you to come back to the office.'

I said no and hung up. I didn't want to see anybody.

The phone rang again, and I sat on the edge of the bed and thought about Edith. She had been, and in my memory she still was, the most beautiful woman I had ever seen.

As soon as the ringing stopped, I snatched up the phone and told the operator I wasn't taking any calls. But she was a real hep woman; she said, 'Not even the police? They're on the wire now.'

'Put them on,' I said. 'If you don't, they'll come over in person, and then you'll miss listening in.'

She suppressed a giggle, and clicked some switches and said, 'Go ahead, Lieutenant Gamble. Here's Mr. Porter now.'

The lieutenant's measured tones marched

against my ear, which was aching no more than the rest of me. 'Mr. Porter, I want you to know that we found the proper match up at Mt. Hilliard. And we've re-examined Banion and Crosley.'

'The dendrologists?'

'I am glad to see you retain some of your sense of humor. So now, as the matter stands, it is certain that you only spent ten to fifteen minutes up at John Five's place, and that you lighted a match while there. Of course, we have only your word, your unsupported word, that you used that match to smoke a cigarette.' He coughed. 'With Henry Lighton as counsel, that might build up into something of a defense.'

'You didn't call me to cheer me up, Lieutenant.'

'Well, no. That's hardly my way. I wanted to tell you, we've obtained an order from a Chicago judge to search your apartment. Cook County officers should be entering around now. If there are any letters there — or other papers, such as newspaper clippings — proving that you knew where your ex-wife was, whom she had married, tell us now.'

I watched the window curtains fluttering. If I jumped out of the window, I'd probably just break my arches, and have to go to the gallows with flat feet. Or death chamber. How did they kill you in this state? I said, 'Lieutenant, there'll be nothing there. I didn't know. I don't suppose I could convince you of that.'

'I'm not much of a man for hypothetical cases,' he said. 'But let's construct one. You admit you didn't like your wife. Your ex-wife, I should say. So if someone else killed her, you'd be inclined to protect him within limits.'

I said, 'If that's a hypothetical case, the supposition that either a Democrat or a Republican will be the next president. Stop playing, Lieutenant. Maybe I'd cover up for a guy like that. I don't know. I've never been privileged to be around any murders before, or any other police work, for that matter. I know that if I was silly enough to cover for a murderer, I'd drop the thing when it looked as if I might incriminate myself.'

'At that time you'd drop it, eh?'

Lieutenant Gamble was probably nodding his head wisely. 'Well, Mr. Porter, let me say that that time has incontrovertibly arrived. Yes. Have a night's rest, Mr. Porter. I'll be talking to you in the morning.' And he hung up.

I started to ask my friend the operator for the name of a doctor who'd get me some sleeping pills. But Gamble maybe could build that into a sign of a guilty conscience. I'd see what a hot tub could do first.

When I turned on the water in the bathtub, it ran just as slowly as you would expect water to run in a hotel in a town the size of Lowndesburg. The night club dining room seemed the only modern part of this dump.

I undressed slowly, hanging my clothes up with the neatness of a man who has been on the road quite a while. The water in the tub was warm, for a blessing. I slid into it, and stretched out. It was a very long tub. The outside was tiled, but I half-suspect that under the tiles there were still lion's-claw feet.

Aches and pains that I hadn't known

were in me began going away. I rested the back of my neck against the warm edge of the tub and stared at my knees, two craggy islands rising sheer from a soapy sea.

I suddenly started chuckling at my own idea. Like most men of my age — thirty in April — I have had my share of uniform wearing and weapon toting. While there are great differences in the armed forces — between, let's say, a marine private landing on a hostile shore, and an air force cadet taking dual-control training in Texas — a few things are common to all. A lack of bathtubs is one of them. Showers, yes — from holes punched in the bottom of an oil drum, to tiled luxuries in permanent BOQs — but bathtubs aren't for the military. Therefore, a man in a tub feels safe, civilian and serene. He might be worrying about love, money or getting fat, but he's not in immediate danger of being killed.

It was a good note to go to bed on. And that was all for the night. I didn't think I could, but I slept soundly, and without dreams, until Lieutenant Gamble opened the door in the morning.

He stood at the foot of my bed, freshly shaved, neatly dressed, urbane as always. 'Up,' he said. 'On your feet. Dressed.'

A uniformed trooper, one I thought I hadn't seen before, was with him. Gamble jerked his chin, and the trooper slid his hand under my pillow, then jerked the bedclothes down. I said 'Hey' in a squawk of protest. But all that happened was that the trooper went over to where I had stacked my clothes. One by one he threw my possessions at me — underwear, socks, shirt, then my pants. He picked up one of my shoes at a time and ran his hand inside, then the shoes came flying at me, too.

I said: 'I may not pay taxes in this state — '

'Your bill paid here?'

'No. I carry — '

Gamble looked at the phone, and the trooper went and picked it up. 'Cashier, please.'

I told Gamble that I carried a credit card, while hotel bills were sent to the firm.

'You're somewhat severed from Hydrol Machines,' the lieutenant told me. 'I talked to Mr. Harvey Planne last night. You'd better pay your bill.'

The trooper said 'Thank you' into the phone. 'He owes nine dollars, even. His money's in his right-hand pants pocket.'

Gamble snapped his finger. 'Nine dollars, Mr. Porter.'

'Thanks for the 'mister.' I wonder if Hitler's stormtroopers were so polite.'

Gamble snapped his fingers. 'Nine dollars, please.'

I was just putting on the pants. I snapped the top button shut and fished out the roll of bills he'd made me take out of my wallet the night before. I gave him a ten-dollar bill.

He said: 'Tester, you got a one?'

The trooper had to unbutton his hip pocket to get his wallet out. He took a bill from it and gave it to me. I rolled it with the others and put them back in my pocket. Then I zipped my pants shut.

'Officer Tester will bring you a receipt later,' Lieutenant Gamble said. 'Now put your shoes on, and your tie and coat if you want to. I don't believe in getting men off balance before I question them.'

'Can I shave?'

'No,' Lieutenant Gamble said. Flatly, infuriatingly.

'All right,' I said. 'I made a grammatical error. May I shave?'

'Still no.'

'I had all night to cut my throat if I wanted to. Or my wrists. Or are you scared I'll assault you and your trooper with a deadly weapon, i.e. a safety razor?'

'I don't know. There's a book. It says don't let a suspect handle a razor. Thinking it over, the book might have been written when straight razors were still the only tool available for whisker removing. Shave, if it means so much to you.'

But the trooper went into the bathroom with me, changed the blade in my razor for me, and took the razor back the minute I was through. He dried the blade before stowing the razor away in my toilet kit.

When we came back out, Lieutenant Gamble had neatly pulled the bedclothes up and was sitting in the room's one chair. He said, 'That's all right, Tester. Go down, pay the bill, have a cup of coffee if you want to. I'll call the coffee shop if I need you.'

'Okay.' He went away without slamming the door, and I was alone with Gamble.

He put that into words. 'Now we're going to talk, man to man. Just the two of us. I've seen a lot more trouble than you have, I'm sure. Let me tell you that the one single thing a man in your position can do is to co-operate with the authorities. In this case, I am the authority to work with, for the moment; pretty soon the district attorney will take over. We have an appointment with him in half an hour.'

'Will my lawyer be there?'

Lieutenant Gamble shrugged. 'That's pretty much up to the D.A.'

'I thought — '

'I know, I know. Your rights. Your rights are to ask for your attorney. To stand mute until you are in the execution chamber. Then they usually talk. My rights — the rights of the authorities — are to take you over to the mortician's, presumably to identify the victim. I can then keep you there, in the presence of the corpse, as long as I want — up to forty-eight hours, I believe. That's cruel and unusual punishment in my eyes, but not in the eyes of the law. I've never done it.'

'You surprise me a little, Lieutenant. I should think you'd be a lawyer instead of a policeman.'

He laughed drily. 'Very astute, Mr. Porter. I married in my third year of college, when I transferred to law school. Inadvertently, my wife had twins a year later.'

'These things happen.'

He nodded. 'Do you mind if I smoke? I know it's before breakfast for you.'

'Go ahead. I rather wish I had you to defend me instead of Henry Lighton.'

Lieutenant Gamble was lighting his cigarette. He blew out the match with vigor, tossed the burnt bit of cardboard into an ashtray, and blew out smoke. 'Whatever you've read in whodunits, whatever you suspect, the average police officer is anxious to get the truth. In that respect, I'm as much your defense attorney as I am your prosecutor.'

Talk, talk, talk. It went on, and I stopped listening. This was a hotel room, more like other hotel rooms than it was different; this was myself, more as I had always been than I was changed; but the man across the room talking his rounded periods was a policeman trying to find out if I was a murderer.

All of last night seemed unreal; all of now was crazy. I'd gone through the looking-glass into a world that should never have been. I said, 'I'd tell you anything, admit to anything, to get out of this.'

'I suppose so,' Lieutenant Gamble said. 'But it's too late for that. You planned to kill Edith Hilliard. You went up there with that in your mind. You had first, very cleverly, used Mac as an alibi; she had written you that her husband owned these hilly woods, that if you came into the valley trying to sell a land-leveler — '

Like a fool, I interrupted: 'A terracer.'

He smiled. 'Decided you do know something about it, after all?' 'I know I saw a terracer in McLane's window.'

With his left hand, Lieutenant Gamble got a package of cigarettes out of his pocket. He tapped it on his knee till a butt rose, pulled the cigarette out with his lips, and used his lighter with his left hand. His right hand remained immobile, on his lap. Presumably, if I were to jump him, a gun would be available to stop me.

'You know that any implement dealer around here would take you to see John Five if you offered him an exceptionally large commission on a . . . terracer? Yeah, a terracer. Who else around here would need one, but Mt. Hilliard? So you were smart. You picked on Mac, an ex-cop, a present hick police chief. You thought — how do I know what a murderer thinks? A man is crazy to murder at all — that since you would be in with the police chief, it would be easy to fool him. Maybe you thought Mac would close the case, confused, and that would be the end of it. Maybe you thought he'd be too anxious to get his commission on your rig to want to annoy you. But, of course, Mac is a policeman first and a money-maker second.'

Smoke rolled lazily out of his mouth. He smiled at me. 'Crime follows a pattern. I'm really not as brilliant as you might think; just experienced. I don't have to read your mind; I just have to have worked on enough similar cases. Actually, criminals are boring; they're so much alike, and the most boring of all are murderers.'

I waved at the smoke with my hand. 'I'm neither a policeman nor a lawyer, but don't you have to dig up a motive?'

He chuckled. 'She wiped you clean, and she ran you under a vacuum cleaner. Then she wrote you and taunted you. The money that you missed so badly she was spending at the dime store; her new man had real dough, yours was to tip a bellboy with.'

'Where do you cops get your talk?' I asked. 'Is there a course in police school on how to talk tough?'

He smiled. 'It's supposed to intimidate the suspect, Porter. I went to college;

would you like me to say a long word for you? A man can stand most anything but laughter; ask any police officer. She taunted you a little too far, and you set her up for a strangling.'

'I think you're the first man I ever heard say the word 'taunt.' I've read it, but I never heard it used out loud.'

He stood up. 'I told you I was a college man. All right. The district attorney is meeting us over at the court. He will have phoned Lighton. What's ahead of you isn't pleasant, but it's legal and it won't kill you. Suspicion of murder, bail refused. Questioned at the state police barracks, driven to the city, held, questioned, driven to the scene of the crime, questioned. Sooner or later they all talk. The sooner the pleasanter, for all parties interested. Stand up.'

I did. He pushed me towards the door. I moved.

Suddenly something whacked me hard, just below my ribs on the left side. My breath went out in a roar, and I put one hand on the bureau to steady myself. I turned.

Lieutenant Gamble was holding a short piece of cloth in his left hand. 'Just a tube of nylon,' he said. 'Full of sand. Sifted sand; a pebble might bruise your skin. Never hit them on the right side; you might bust an appendix.'

My breath was coming back. 'Mine's out.'

'You've got guts,' Gamble said. 'But the liver's on the right side, too. I had to show you I can get tough. Friendly, tough; it's all one to me. All I want is a confession.'

I rubbed my side. 'Last night you seemed to think I was innocent.'

Lieutenant Gamble looked gloomy. 'That was last night. I spent the night trying to turn up any other possible suspect. I didn't. So now you're guilty . . . I have that much respect for my own ability. If there'd been anyone else, I'd have heard of him by now. Let's go.'

6

The Justice of the Peace room was across from City Hall on the other side of the square from the hotel. It was a room that should have been, maybe had been, a candy store or a shoeshine parlor; narrow and long. A set of twelve legal-looking books occupied a glass-front case, and an American flag drooped behind a yellow oak desk. The J.P. needed a haircut.

I was introduced to the district attorney as though we were going to be friends: Mr. Norton Prince. He had been to college, too, with a man named Henry Porter, from Chicago. I said it was a common name and a big city.

He nodded, respecting the wisdom of my observation, and turned to Henry Lighton. 'We might as well get this over with.'

Henry Lighton said we might as well, and we did. I was to be turned over to the sheriff and held for the grand jury.

Lighton applied for bail, on the grounds that I was being held on circumstantial evidence. Mr. Norton Prince cited a statute, and the J.P. denied bail.

Lieutenant Gamble took my arm, said 'Hold out your hands,' and snapped cuffs on me. 'Are you the sheriff?' I inquired.

'All state police officers are authorized to act as deputy sheriffs. They passed a law ten years ago. Right, Mr. Lighton?'

Lighton said, 'Don't bother me. I'm thinking up angles about false arrest. About malfeasance based on malice.'

Lieutenant Gamble said, 'I do a neat, clean job. No angles, Mr. Lighton.'

Mr. Norton Prince said he would buy Henry a cup of coffee. 'We'll see you later, Lieutenant, Mr. Porter.'

Gamble took my elbow. 'I'll lock you up at Mac's dog house. Prince wants to take you up to Mt. Hilliard later.'

He pushed me ahead of him out on the street. Lowndesburg had turned out to see a real live murderer. Two state cops were holding the populace back. He shoved me at one of them. 'Put him in the lockup, Marske, and get someone to sign for him. I'm going for coffee.'

Marske's pal pulled a gun, and Marske grabbed my elbow. 'Out of the way, folks.'

The folks broke, let us through, and closed in behind us. I didn't know if the drawn gun was for me or the crowd; the trooper holding it shot his sullen eyes in all directions. Marske was reasonably gentle, pushing me ahead of him; and when we got to the steps leading down into Mac's police station, the pal with the gun stayed at the top of them. The office was empty except for one man.

I was meeting all kinds of law officers. This one was neat in khaki pants and shirt, and his badge had come from a dime store; it just said, 'Police' without any rank or the name of any city. He had lost half of one arm, his right one, and his left hand held a ring of keys.

He unlocked one of the cells behind Mac's desk, and Marske took my handcuffs off with a key from his pocket. I'd learned something: all state police handcuffs worked off any state police key.

Marske said, 'Lieutenant wants a receipt for him.'

The one-armed turnkey grunted. 'Sure. We're likely to lose him in here. Which lieutenant, Gamble?'

As he said it, he unlocked the iron-barred gate behind Mac's desk. He nodded for me to go through. 'Sit in any cell, son, or stand around the aisle. We turned all our drunks out an hour ago.'

He sat down at Mac's desk while I watched from the aisle of the four-cell lockup. He pulled paper towards him, held it down with the stump of his right arm, and wrote clumsily with his one hand. 'I used ta be on the state force,' he said. 'Sergeant Knowles. Heard of me?'

Marske said politely: 'I think so, Sergeant.'

'Just mister, now. I'm sort of jail janitor here. I sleep back there, through that other door, and I fetch the meals when the prisoners need 'em — and we got prisoners — and I answer the phone.'

'Tough,' Marske said. He read the paper that was handed him, read it carefully.

'Not so tough,' Knowles said. 'I'm on half pay from the state, too. Not bad.'

Marske said something polite, and marched out. Knowles got up from McLane's desk and came over near the bars. 'Had breakfast, Mr. Porter?'

'No.'

He thought. 'I got a pot of coffee on the burner in my room, a couple of doughnuts. If those'll do you, you won't have to wait. Otherwise, I gotta send for the day cop, the traffic cop, to come watch you while I go out. Chief McLane decided to leave him on the traffic, thought I could hold you. How about the chow?'

'The coffee and doughnuts'll do fine, thanks. But why watch me? I'm not going anyplace.'

Mr. Knowles said: 'When I have a prisoner, someone stays with him. Supposing the building caught on fire, supposing you had a heart attack? You can't get out, can't even get to a phone.'

I said I was sorry. 'You're a pretty decent guy.'

'I'm a washed-up one. I won't say that when I was a big muckamuck running around in a tailor-made sergeant's suit, I didn't have too much pride for my own good . . . I'll get that coffee.'

He brought it back and handed it through the bars to me. Then he handed me one of those folding TV tables, tray first, then the legs. I fetched a stool out of one of the cells and sat in the corridor. He sat in the side chair, not at McLane's desk. He lighted a cigarette just the way Lieutenant Gamble had done, but in his case it was necessary since he had only one arm. That police trick must have come in handy when he lost the other one.

'I got a little radio if you need to pass the time.'

'I think I'm only going to be here an hour. They're taking me up to Mt. Hilliard to see the place where — well, you know. I didn't kill her, before you ask.'

'Wasn't going to,' Knowles said. He blew out smoke.

'Incidentally, I lost my arm when a car turned over, before you ask.'

'I wasn't going to.'

We both laughed. Underground as we

were, the noises of the town were soothing and distant. The one window in the cell block was above my head, and just at ground level, apparently. It was closed and barred, and the noise came down the stairwell from the City Hall lawn.

He said: 'That damned Gamble asking for a receipt!' The stump of his arm jerked once, as though a nerve hurt him. He put the cigarette in his mouth and rubbed his short arm.

I said: 'Yesterday morning I didn't have a care in the world.'

'I was stashed up behind a bunch of trees, watching the highway, smoking a cigarette. These guys came along at ninety per. I took after them, and five minutes later I'd put the cruiser into a ditch.'

'Life.'

'And myself into a pension,' he said. 'The hell it's life. I was due to go off watch in twenty minutes ... We got a visitor.'

I thought it would be Lieutenant Gamble come to get me, and I think Knowles did, too, because he stayed in his chair. But it was Andy McLane. A black cotton dress showed under the same tweed coat she'd worn last night.

Knowles jumped out of his chair. 'Hi, Andy. Sure nice to see you.'

She said, 'Hi, Knowlesy; hi, Paul. Okay to visit with your prisoner, Knowlesy?'

'You know better than that,' Knowles said. 'His attorney of record, Henry Lighton, has a right to see him; nobody else.' He considered. 'But that Gamble, and his receipt. I was a sergeant when he was still a rookie. How's a small-town clown like me gonna know that a prisoner's not supposed to have visitors? G'wan. Only I better sit between you.' He grabbed up his chair with his one arm and swung it right around the bars. 'I'll sit down, and you can both talk over my head. Don't try and touch him, don't try and pass anything to him.'

She got up close to where Knowles was sitting, and now she was only two or three feet from me. 'Gramps was worried about you. He sent me down here to see if there's anything you need.'

'You're the damndest family,' I said.

'Yesterday I was admiring how well you got along with your father. Last night I had a big shouting match with him, and five minutes later you were walking across the square with me.'

'Well, Dad's all right, and I'm crazy about him, but Gramps is the real brain in our family. He thinks Dad shouldn't have called in the state police.'

Between us, Knowles grunted. As though remembering him, Andy said, 'Got a cigarette for me, Knowlesy?'

He grunted again, and got the pack out from under his badge. He did his act of making a single cigarette climb out of the package, and held it out to her, smiling.

Andy hesitated a moment, and then reached. But not for the cigarette. She grabbed Knowles's only wrist in her two hands, and twisted. Knowles came back against the bars. Andy was crying again. She said, 'Paul! Hit him.'

Knowles was making absolutely no effort to get away — which maybe he couldn't, if Andy had ever taken a Red Cross course in life saving. But he wasn't trying to yell either, and that he certainly could have done.

I did nothing, and after a moment, Andy let go. Knowles bent over, giving her a free shot at the back of his neck, and picked up his cigarettes. 'Here's your butt, Andy.'

She took it, and he lighted it for her with a wooden match and his fingernail, turned, and held the package through the bars. I had cigarettes of my own, but I took one.

We all three blew smoke at each other for a while, without anyone meeting anyone else's eyes. Finally Knowles said: 'You can't do things like that, Andy. Some people can, but you can't.'

Andy said, 'I suppose so,' her voice completely dreary. 'But Paul — '

'I know, I know,' Knowles said. 'You can't sock an unarmed friend, and Paul probably couldn't strangle his wife. I get a lot of time to think, back there in my janitor's room, listening to the drunks sing 'Sparrow in the Treetop'. It gives me lots of time to think.'

'Knowlesy — '

'It's forgotten. You think I'd go out of

my way to report this, or anything else, to Gamble?'

Andy said, 'Or to my Dad.'

'Mac gave me this job. I'm obliged to him.' His jaws moved as though he wanted to spit.

'Who rates higher,' I said, 'a sergeant of state police or a captain on the city force?'

'That's a damned fool question.'

I suppose it was. At any rate, he didn't give me an answer. And I didn't bother to ask Mac when he came in a minute later, with a dirty look at Andy for hanging around a jailbird like me, a dirty look at Knowles for letting her, and no look at all for me.

The two tree men, Banion and Crosley were with him. Mac said, 'Stand over there and raise your right hands.' They did. 'Do you swear to uphold the laws of this city and state and the Constitution of the United States?' and they both nodded.

Mac unlocked a desk drawer, took out two badges and handed them over. Knowles grunted for no reason I could think of, until I noticed that these were much more expensive shields than the one the turnkey wore. I wondered what kept Knowles from greasing the steps down to the office some night when Mac was due to walk down them.

'All right,' said Mac, 'take him up to the court room, boys.' He turned. 'Open the lockup, Knowles.'

Andy was peering into her compact mirror, straightening her lipstick, dabbing powder under her eyes. 'I'm going with you, Paul.'

Mac said: 'No.'

Andy didn't hear him. The temporary cops each took an elbow, and we went out. I didn't say goodbye to Knowles; I didn't think it would help him with his boss to appear too friendly with me, and he needed the job.

For once there was no mob around the jail. With nothing to see, they'd drifted away, maybe to watch the state officers eat their breakfasts.

I said, 'I thought you lads were dendrologists, not cops.'

Banion said, 'I took a forestry degree. They give you a course in law enforcement in case you go into the Forest

Service. Anyway, Mr. Hilliard is worried you'll get loose. What you did to Mrs. Hilliard he doesn't want done to him. So he lent us to Mac.'

Andy was ambling alongside us. She said, 'Danny, you look like a policeman, anyway.'

Banion said, 'Don't know how to take that, Andy. Say, they're changing the bill at the Metro today. Wanta go tonight?'

'No, thanks.' She managed a smile.

The other temporary cop, Crosley, said, 'Our prisoner's cut you out, Dan.'

Dan Banion looked at me. 'This dude? That on the level, Andy?'

Andy didn't answer. Banion shook his head and tightened his grip on my arm. 'You ought to get someone with more staying power. This guy's got as much liberty left as a mouse with his tail in a trap.'

'He's got Henry Lighton,' Crosley said.

Banion said, 'Yeah, sure. That guy. Anyway, don't escape, Porter, or Crosley and I'll have to chase you. You really got the boss scared.'

I didn't feel like chatting, but my ego

demanded a show of nonchalance. 'How come John Five had to send you boys down to be deputized? Doesn't he have private cops as well as private foresters?'

Crosley said, 'Sure, do you think we're cheap? They're watchmen, though, not private cops, and John Five doesn't even call them that; they're fire guards. Which puts them under Danny Banion here and me, and so we're the ones he chose.'

'I see. I'd kind of like to meet John Five.'

We were circling the courthouse, going around to the front door. Banion looked across the municipal lawn and said: 'Here come the ghouls,' indicating citizens converging on us. We all started walking faster, and Danny Banion added, 'You'll see John Five all right. He'll be at your trial.'

Andy said, 'Maybe there won't be a trial.'

Still holding on to my arm, Crosley shook his head. 'Oh, there'll be a trial all right. Henry Lighton always has a trial. He usually wins it, but going without it would be like asking a Barrymore to rehearse and then not give the show.'

'Crosley's got the education,' Banion said. 'He's Yale School of Forestry. Me, I'm just Syracuse.'

We went up the broad steps and into the courthouse. Up more steps and through a wide door that a bailiff in a neat blue uniform held open for us, and we were in a regular courtroom, complete with judge on the bench, a jury waiting to hear a trial, lawyers, spectators, defendant. Nearly as I could tell, the trial had been halted while Mr. Henry Lighton and the Honorable Norton Prince, D.A. argued about me, because the judge seemed testy.

He said, 'All right, all right, Mr. Lighton, here's your man now. You applied for habeas corpus, and the court has granted it, the police have complied.' He peered. 'Who are you men? Where's Police Chief McLane?'

'Sulking in his tent, no doubt,' Henry Lighton said. He chuckled.

'We're special deputies, your honor,' Crosley said.

'All right, all right. You're Paul Porter, young man?'

'Yes, sir.'

'You're admitted to ten thousand dollars' bail. Go over to the clerk there, and sign the papers he gives you. Your attorney has stipulated that you will not leave the county. Agreeable to you?'

'Yes, s — your honor.' I didn't know much about bail, but I knew the lining of my own wallet: no ten grand. But maybe if I sold my car, it would bring enough to pay the premium on a bond. I'd held bonded jobs, and I knew about that kind of bond. Maybe this was similar.

Henry Lighton tapped me on the arm. His eyes were glowing with a deep fire I hadn't seen in them before, and he seemed ridiculously happy. 'Over here,' he said.

I followed him over to the low desk under the bench. 'This is Mr. deVries,' Henry Lighton said. 'Clerk of this venerable court, and a jim dandy of a cribbage player.'

I bowed, and tried to smile at the old clerk.

Henry Lighton went on: 'And you know Mr. Gray, of course,' and I turned from the clerk to — of all people — Andy's grandfather. I hadn't seen him there. Even after looking at him, I could hardly see him; he was wrapped in overcoats, mufflers and shawls till it didn't seem likely he could move. Andy appeared from behind and gave him support. 'Gramps, you shouldn't — '

'Do me good. Haven't seen the old courthouse in a spell. Always surprised me it stood up. Hank here — ' He indicated deVries. ' — his uncle sold the county the rock, an' I always calculated he kinda cheated. Should have fallen down in the first hard freeze.'

The court clerk chuckled and said, 'I'll be up to whip you at pinochle, cribbage, you name it, soon's this session of court's over. You sign here, Mr. Porter. Maybe you better read it first. Says you're remanded to custody Mr. Gray, your bondsman, an' he forfeits his worldly goods if you decamp. Better keep on lurin' him, Andrea; ten thousand dollars is a mite of money to lose.'

A county full of bucolic characters. I signed the papers and we went out in a little group, Henry Lighton, Mr. Gray, Andy, me. Henry and Andy were helping the old gentleman. I said I didn't know what had happened. Lighton laughed. 'You don't have to. All that happened is that I'm a much better lawyer than Norton Prince. I got the judge to reduce the booking to suspicion of complicity.'

'But Mr. Gray — '

Mr. Gray cackled. 'Just money, son. You aren't the running-away type. And this'll fair put Otto in a tizzy, which is where I like to see him. Might make him so mad he'll move outta my house.'

Andy said: 'Gramps, you'd miss him.'

'Didn't say I wouldn't. Henry, you drive me home. That damn car of Andy's is full of drafts.'

The good people of Lowndesburg weren't used to seeing me without cops on my arms and wrists. There were people around the courthouse, but they paid no attention to me; though two men, obviously reporters, made a dive for Henry Lighton.

Softly as possible, Andy murmured, 'Let's get away.'

116

Her car was across the lawn, illegally parked on the wrong side of the street, but who gives a ticket to the police chief's daughter's car?

She said, 'You don't want to drive, do you?' and didn't wait for an answer while she got behind the wheel. She started before the motor was warm and nearly stalled at the first traffic light. But she viciously pumped gas to the motor and went on through the gray streets of Lowndesburg.

'I'd like to ask something,' I said.

'Sure.'

'Who's watching the store? Your father's out police chiefing, you're chauffeuring fugitives; who sells feed and seed?'

Her eyes were on the road ahead of her 'What's it to you? I understand you're unemployed, so even if some shoplifter steals that land-leveler, it isn't your business.'

'In the first place, it's a terracer, not a land-leveler. In the second place, I'm not unemployed. I'm on indefinite leave of absence. Till I clear myself.'

117

Andy said, 'Oh. Your Mr. Planne took the trouble to call us and tell us he wasn't standing behind any checks you wanted to cash. A good friend.'

'A boss,' I said. I looked out at the streets. Yesterday had been spring, but now winter had come back; the light was cold and gray. One of those late snows was probably about to powder the Midwest. They don't do any harm to the crops. You have to know about such things when your business depends on farm prosperity.

It seemed a great many years since I had had any business to depend on anything.

'Andy,' I said. 'I seem to have asked this before, but what's it all about? I don't mean my being accused of murder — I understand that — but all the rest? Your grandfather, Henry Lighton . . . you, for that matter? You never saw me before yesterday.'

She turned her gaze away from the windshield a moment to look at me. Then she turned back, carefully twisted the car into the curb, and stopped. She left the motor running, for the heater.

'Gramps said I wasn't to answer any of your questions.'

I said, 'Oh. Just go along and be pushed in and out of jail whenever some member of your family feels like exercise.'

'If you think I'm helping to frame you, get out.'

She reached across me and twisted my door handle. Her weight was across my lap for the moment. 'Go on, get out.'

'Keep your chemise on.'

She said, 'Women don't wear them anymore,' and started up again. This was more like the Andy McLane I knew. I felt a little better.

'Where are you taking me?'

'Home.'

'Maybe your grandfather will answer a few of my questions.'

She said, 'Maybe,' and slowed down to let a car pass us. Nobody in it seemed to give me a second glance.

I rode along in a daze. I was a pawn in a game whose rules — if there were any rules — I didn't know. I was a puck in an ice hockey match. I didn't seem to have done anything but get kicked around, shoved, advised and then not asked if I was going to take the advice.

She stopped in front of Mr. Gray's big house and we got out. I said: 'You must be the first police chief's daughter in history to help bail a man out of her father's hoosegow.'

Now that she was on her own — her grandfather's — lawn, she was more at ease. She reached up and patted my cheek. 'Haven't you heard about Dr. Freud? I'm in rivalry with my father.'

'That's for boys, not women,' I said. I didn't have to bend far to reach her lips. They were firm and cold from the air.

But after a moment it was plain that she knew the trick most nice women learn — learn young, if I remember my high school days correctly — of letting a man kiss them without committing themselves. I couldn't tell whether she was just being patient with me, or with herself, waiting for her heart to tell her whether she really wanted to kiss me. So I let her go.

She said, 'Go see Grandpa. I'll make some coffee and bring it.' Her voice said nothing had happened, but her eyes were bright, or maybe my ego made me think so.

In the daytime, the house was only slightly less gloomy than it had been the night before.

The old man in the conservatory looked as if he hadn't moved since we drank sherry with him.

He was listening to the radio. Somebody was banging away at the administration. Old Mr. Gray looked at me, smiled and slowly reached out and turned a knob. The sound died away. He said, 'Half man and half horse.'

I must have looked sufficiently blank, because he cackled, and said. 'A cen-a-taur. Awful pun, and not original, anyway . . . How was jail?'

'I'm out on ten thousand bond. Your money.'

His fuzzy eyebrows crawled up the drought-cracked river bed that was his forehead. 'That's all right, boy. Don't go on thanking me. You embarrass me with all them kind words. Down, boy. Stop kissing me.'

'You don't know me. And don't give me that line about Andy being interested in me. While we were going up for the hearing, she was flirting with one of John Five's private rangers. Anyway, anybody with a half a good eye could see you wouldn't have to buy her a husband.'

'That's right, she could have any man in town now.'

The cracked old voice came down hard on the word 'now.' But maybe it was just age's inability to control any of its functions, even the voice . . .

He went on: 'Think I caught cold, goin' down to that durned courthouse. Drafty old dump, ain't it? Did I tell you, the fella that's clerk of the court, his uncle . . . '

'You told me. What do you mean, Andy can get any man in town now?'

'Jest what I said. Best-lookin' gal in the county now. When Mrs. John Five was alive, she could have her choice of Lowndes County's fellas, of course. A looker from way back.'

The image of Edith came back on me. Desirable, alluring . . . but then, I would add, unattainable, and she would have been the perfect woman. It was when you got her that you got trouble.

Mr. Gray said, 'You all right, son?'

Through the red haze that had bowed my head, I heard the front door close. I said, 'Where did Henry Lighton go?'

'Back down to his office fer a spell. He'll be back to talk to you . . . Thinking about yer wife got you down?'

'It's hard to realize she's dead. Lieutenant Gamble was going to make me look at the body, but so far he hasn't.'

The old man said, 'Thank God for small favors.'

Sitting there suddenly became impossible. I jumped to my feet. 'I came in here to find out why I'm being pushed all over Lowndesburg — in jail, out of jail — but the talk got away from me.'

'I'm an old man, son. I ramble. First sign of senility.'

'You're about as senile as I am.'

'I'm eighty, son. Never had a child till Andy's mother was born — Lissa we called her — and that was forty-five years ago. Was thirty-five then. Apple of my eye, boy, till she went up to the city to have a career an' met Mac.'

'We're rambling again. Why did you bail me out?'

'Don't shout at me. Got good hearing, fer all my age.'

'Why — did you — bail me — out?'

A car started up outside. The door must have been Andy going away.

Old Mr. Gray said: 'Don't believe in keeping nothing penned. Not dog, nor fox, nor man. John Five, now, he has his boys breed foxes up there on the Mount, and turn one loose fer him an' his bosses to chase. On-nacheral, I calls it.'

'One minute your grammar's as good as a college professor's, the next minute you're playing the country clown.'

He cackled his horrible laugh again. 'You gettin' around to saying I killed Edith Hilliard, Paul? I couldn't strangle a new-hatched chicken.'

He brought his claws up in front of him and flexed and un-flexed them a few times. Then his eyes brightened. 'About time for my morning glass of sherry.'

'I heard Andy go out.'

'Mebee she had to go downtown to buy

a fresh bottle . . . There's a car coming, now.'

'Will you please tell me why you bailed me out?'

'Nope,' he said. 'That's not Andy's car. Don't know whose it is, an' my hearing's magnificent.'

Whoever it was knew the house well enough to enter without the use of the front door bell, knew it well enough to know where to find human companionship, or at least that of Mr. Gray. Masculine steps strode bravely towards us, and I felt apprehensive.

That old devil sensed it. 'Scared, Paul? Want to take a powder?'

I saved what was left of my dignity by not telling him to go to hell. It was only Henry Lighton, my learned counsel.

He said: 'I've been down talking to Otto and Lieutenant Gamble. They released your car, Paul; you'll have to drive me back downtown.'

I nodded. 'I've been trying to get Mr. Gray here to tell me why he bailed me out.'

'The study of the mouths of donated

horses is a notoriously unrewarding occupation,' Lighton said.

'He never saw me before. For all he knows, I'm going away and forfeiting his ten thousand dollars.'

Henry Lighton laughed. 'You wouldn't get across the state line; you probably wouldn't even get to the county line. Our lieutenant, the good Gamble, is unhappy . . . It wasn't his fumble, it was Norton Prince's. With the growth of the big corporations it is harder and harder to find a good lawyer to stay home and run for district attorney.'

Old Mr. Gray said: 'Makes it hard on a real fine trained policeman like Gamble.'

'You're right,' said Lighton. 'Would make an interesting article, if I were thinking of becoming literary, and you know I just might. The rise in training of the police officer, accompanied by the fall in training of the lawyer available for Political offices, and the cause of it all . . . '

'I'd like to read that. There's been changes in business, too,' Mr. Gray said. 'In the twenties, the salesman'd be a big fella, full of beefsteak an' bootleg, and if he brought an engineer along from the office, it'd be some measly little wretch that he'd stable down at the railroad hotel. Nowadays . . . '

My hand hit the table hard. I shook it, feeling it sting even through the very real anger that was shaking me. 'It's no time to exchange rural philosophy. I'm facing a murder charge!'

Lighton said: 'Have no fear; Henry Lighton is here. I made a monkey out of Norton Prince this morning. I can do it again, on call.'

Old Mr. Gray just sat blinking his eyes, a tree sloth awakened from a deep sleep.

I said, 'Henry, I don't want to get off on a technicality. I want my name cleared, my job back.'

He looked at me, and smiled. It wasn't a smile calculated to bring joy and happiness into my life. 'You'll be cleared the way I think is best.'

'If you don't mind, it's my life.' It sounded school-boyish and weak as I said it. 'I don't want to go to trial for something I didn't do.'

Henry Lighton said, 'Until you've been tried, dismissed, and the law of double jeopardy sets in, this will be hanging over you all your life.'

'Or until the real murderer's caught.'

Lighton shrugged. 'Then hire a detective, not a lawyer.' He turned his tweedy shoulders away from me. 'Mr. Gray, consider this. Can it be that the trend is away from the office man, the fellow who looks things up in books, and towards the field man, the fellow — learned enough — who uses books only occasionally and as a minor tool? The policeman and the engineer, for instance, though — '

The front door opened and closed. I left them there, and went to look for Andy.

7

She was in the front room of the house, opening a bottle of sherry, just as her grandfather had predicted, but she was not alone. Danny Banion was with her, in his sturdy forester's clothes, still wearing his special policeman's badge. He was talking: ' . . . could have knocked me over with a feather. Turning that guy loose!'

Andy's head was bent down over the bottle, as though she were struggling with the cork. But it was just a bottle of domestic sherry, the kind that is sealed with a simple metal cap. Her shiny hair had fallen forward, and I could not see her face.

She spoke with difficulty. 'I don't believe Paul Porter's guilty.'

'You're in love,' Danny Banion said. 'I don't know why, but you are! Come out of the clouds and use your head. Stands to reason, no guy but John Five would put up with the way that dame behaved.

129

Believe me, I've had the night watch up at Mt. Hilliard, going around the house, checking the doors and windows. I've heard them at it; it sounded like she charged John Five ten grand for a kiss, and God knows what for anything more! So any real man, not John Five, but a real guy, would have — '

Andy's head came up; I don't think she saw me, but I stepped back into the wide hall. 'Go to hell, Danny Banion. Go to — Mt. Hilliard. You ought to be there!'

He said: 'John Five wants a watch around the clock; I got the night du — That stuff doesn't matter. Come to your senses, Andy. I'm quitting this job, going back into the Forest Service! C'mon with me, kid. It'll be a swell job!'

Andy started to cry, not politely like a movie actress, but loudly, as though she was at the end of her patience, of her very strength. I made as little noise as possible going out.

My car was at the curb. I had an extra set of keys my pocket, but I didn't need them. Henry Lighton had left keys in the ignition, the ones taken from me at the jail . . . Safe Lowndesburg, happy Lowndesburg where nothing so naughty as a car thief would dare to operate.

I didn't know where the county lines were, and if I went out in the country I was likely to cross one, thus forfeiting Mr. Gray's bail. So I headed downtown. Even in a small place like Lowndesburg, there ought to be one bar low enough for the customers to mind their own business.

I found it, finally on the south end of town, near the highway. There was a shed for ice trucks nearby, and a filling station in front of the bar. Everything needed paint. The inevitable juke box was playing, and two couples sat in the booths; there were three men at the bar. Everybody looked a little shabby and undersized. I got myself a rye highball and carried it to one of the booths. After a minute the bartender followed me, and put a bowl of pretzels on the table; he didn't seem to have looked at me.

Now I was alone, out of the dreary weather, away from the curious people; now I ought to be able to think. There was some easy solution to my problem. I was a big-city man, a successful man; surely I could out-think these hicks and rubes.

So I sipped my highball ... and nothing came.

Maybe I ought to ask the bartender for a pencil and paper, I thought, and make a list of everybody I knew in Lowndesburg, and eliminate them one by one. But the trouble was, I knew hardly anyone there, and in all probability it was someone I didn't know who had killed Edith.

The only thing I was sure of was that old Mr. Gray knew all about it, or he wouldn't have been so damned helpful. But certainly he hadn't killed Edith; and also, just as certainly, I couldn't get him to tell me anything he didn't want to tell me. I wasn't as smart as he was, and any use of force would just kill him.

The juke box changed from one rock and roll number to another; a very slight change.

The front door opened, and a woman came in, as well as a burst of damp, chilly air. She started for the bar, then turned and walked over to my booth and sat down opposite me. I was surprised. Things were going on in Mac's town he didn't know about. B-women, yet.

Not a bad-looking B-woman, either. Maybe not my type, but smart-enough-looking; clean white blouse under a red chamois jacket, hair permanented — or maybe naturally wavy, not too much makeup on.

I said: 'I'm sorry, miss. I'm just sitting here thinking. I'm not in the mood for romps and frolics.'

She said: 'Wouldn't think you would be, Mr. Porter. Did that pug-faced police chief beat you up?'

It wasn't a vulgar voice; it had been to high school. But then, who hasn't? But it was a little high-pitched.

'You know who I am.' After I said it, I gave myself a medal for elocution and extemporaneous speaking. That was a truly brilliant remark, and I am as proud of it now as I was then.

'Lou, the bartender, called me when you came in. He thought you might like to talk to me.'

'I'm not in need of comfort.'

'God,' she said, 'you're stuffy. No wonder your wife left you. Mister, I don't have to pick up dudes in a beer joint. But seeing that you and I don't like McLane any better than anybody else does, maybe I could talk to you. I'm Janey Dandler, by the way.'

The name, of course, didn't mean a thing to me, but I seemed to have an ally. I began to brighten. She didn't look like a silver lining, but she didn't look like a dark cloud either. 'Drink, Miss Dandler?'

'Sure.' She turned her head and her voice went up an octave, cutting across the juke box racket. 'Dry martini, Lou.'

His lips shaped, 'Sure, Janey,' but the rock and roll kept me from hearing him.

I said, 'I thought rock and roll was dead.'

'It just smells that way,' she said. 'I figure you didn't kill Mrs. John Five.'

'Nice of you, but how do you make that out?'

'If you had, Chief McLane would have pinched somebody else. That copper never made a right collar in his life.'

She must have learned that talk from television. Maybe a new generation of underworld will grow up, talking the way the magazine writers of the '30's thought they ought to talk, as TV actors talk now: life following art.

Lou came and put a martini glass in front of her, poured her drink, and left her a generous dividend in the mixing glass.

I put a pile of coins on the table, but he shook his head. 'On the house. You can buy the next one. You ain't sore because I called Janey, are you?'

'Of course not, Lou.'

He said, 'Swell,' and went back behind the bar.

'You're popular here,' I told Janey.

'Lou is Red's brother,' she said obscurely, and drank half her cocktail. Her lips pursed in and out once in acknowledgement of its strength, while I tried to remember if I knew anyone named Red. 'That don't mean a thing to you, does it? Red and I were engaged. Now he's in the VA hospital, with a ruptured kidney.'

'A little light is penetrating my head.'

'You talk stuffed up,' she said. 'You probably can't help it. My old man owns the taxi company. I'm one of the two dispatchers. My sister-in-law and I switch around, night and day; I'm night this week. Red was one of our drivers.'

I kept my stuffed-up mouth from talking, since it seemed to annoy her. She drank the rest of her drink, without reaction this time, and started pouring her dividend.

'There's an old souse in this town,' she said. 'I guess more than one, but this particular guy — his name is Freddy Hughes — he gets a pension from some company he used to work for. He cashes it here, Lou keeps half of it, Freddy drinks up the other half. The rest of the month, Lou gives him so much a day for beer and groceries.'

'It sounds like Mr. Hughes has it made.'

She gulped the dividend. I raised a finger for Lou, pointed at Janey's glass, and mine. He nodded.

Janey said, 'You think we're dirt, don't

you? Night cab drivers like Red, bartenders like Lou, drunks like Freddy Hughes. 'Mr. Hughes!' 'A little light is penetrating my cranium!''

'Head, not cranium,' I said. 'Don't make it any worse than it is.'

'Sorry.' Janey looked at me. 'Like I said, maybe you can't help it. Anyway, while Freddy was still riding high, couple of months ago, good deal of money in his pocket, he passed out at the Red Rooster, a joint on the edge of town. They phoned for a cab, and I sent Red out there. He took Freddy home. I mean, I know he did, because he said so. Only, the next morning, McLane's traffic cop, Jess Fencher, found Freddy in a vacant lot with his dough gone.'

The juke box, for once, was silent. I nodded, and we were both still while Lou brought us fresh drinks. I tapped the coins and told Lou to take out for a drink for himself. 'Don't use the stuff when I'm working,' he said. 'Nice story, ain't it?'

I had forgotten Red was his brother. I nodded, and he went back behind the bar, looking unhappy.

Janey said, 'The rest of it won't last this drink out. McLane was still beating on Red, trying to get a confession, when a guy over in Millsville, just a passing no-good who peddles thread and stuff to little stores, gets drunk enough to start bragging about the neat trick he pulled here. Seems Freddy came to, and was trying to make it downtown when this salesman runs into him.'

I sipped my drink. 'I don't see where I stand.'

She leaned across the table, her martini forgotten.

'You're not trash, mister, like Red and me. You got a fancy car and fancy friends. The word is, you're out on ten grand bail; you could melt all my family and all Red's family including Lou's license here, and all our friends, and we wouldn't make half that. I'll bet McLane didn't even beat you, once.'

One of the men at the bar got up and came over to put a nickel in the damned juke box. We were both quiet while I thought it over. The music started again, but this time it was just a woman singing in some quiet rhythm.

'Make a beef, Mr. Porter,' Janey said. 'Make a stink. For the rich, the law listens. False arrest, whatever — you got Henry Lighton, they'll listen to him. Break that McLane down for me, mister.'

'And then?'

'Then we get a decent police chief here, we get to live a little. Listen, I know you'll get off anyway; Henry Lighton never lost a case yet. But do it the hard way, that's all I ask. Stand up and yell!'

She seemed on the level. I said, 'That'll heal Red's kidney?'

'It'll make him feel like a man again. How do you think a guy feels, taking a shellacking, and then scared to complain about it?'

Surprisingly, I answered that. 'I know. When I got out on bail today, I felt just that way. I'll do what I can, Janey, but — there's nothing I *can* do. I wouldn't kid you. I don't know anyone in Lowndes-burg, and without knowing anyone how can I find out who killed Ed — who killed Mrs. Hilliard? That's why I'd take the easy way out. The Henry Lighton way.

You're not asking me to take a chance on being convicted of murder, are you?'

She made a sort of sideways sweep with her hand. 'Hell, I don't know what I'm asking.' Growing up among the taxicabs hadn't refined her overmuch. 'You're not such a bad joe. Before you ask me, I don't know who killed Mrs. John Five.'

'Otto McLane?'

She made the gesture again, the throwing-away movement. 'I'd like to think so.'

I said: 'This is none of your business. But his father-in-law went my bail, and is paying Henry Lighton's fee. I'm not as rich as you thought me.'

Her eyes lit up. She turned towards the bar and whistled, undoubtedly a whistle she'd learned to summon sleeping cab drivers. Lou's head snapped up, and he came towards us at once.

She said: 'Old Mr. Gray greased Paul here out of the lockup. He's paying his lawyer. Whatya think?'

Lou got that same delighted look in his eye. Then it died. 'Naw. Why should Mac kill her? How would he even know her?'

140

'They're on a Civil Defense Committee together,' Janey said.

Lou said 'Aw' in a disgusted way. 'Naw. John Five had her bumped, of course.' He turned and went back to the bar, a very businesslike man.

I stared at Janey. 'Now, that's a dandy sort of suggestion right out of the clear blue sky.'

'You're making noises like a stuffed shirt again,' she said. 'I suppose because John Five's got money, he wouldn't kill anybody? I suppose the rich don't spit when they got a mouthful? I suppose — '

I cut in before she told me the rest of the things she supposed the rich didn't do. I was beginning to wonder if any of her story was true. On the other hand, I hated to doubt it, since it made her my friend. I wasn't overburdened with pals.

I said: 'Just because John Five's rich doesn't mean he murders his wives, does it?'

'Look at it with a little logic. She was a lousy wife to you, wasn't she? No reason to suppose she wouldn't be a lousy wife to him. You, she can leave, and what would it mean to you? A few lousy grand. She leaves him, and — zowie — any jury gives her a few zillion bucks of alimony. Especially looking like she did.'

'Not a female jury.'

Janey looked gloomily at the table. 'Especially a bunch of hens. Guys don't understand dames. They wouldn't be jealous of her. Especially the kind of bridge-playing clucks who like jury duty. Naw. They figure next week, maybe tomorrow, they're gonna buy a new bottle of face cream, or maybe a girdle, that makes them look just like Mrs. John Five. Yeah, she'd of got a big alimony, all right.'

The cabman's delight lifted her head and sighed a deep, heartfelt sigh. 'I wish I had a crack at that kind of money.'

'John Five was up in the city when she was killed.'

Janey almost spat at me. 'Says he. Says Otto Goddam McLouse McLane. How d'we know? And anyways, John Five wouldn't do it himself. He's got a private army up there! It's half as big as the whole state police force, almost. He'd have one of them do it.'

My head was shaking. 'All right,' I said. 'I'll go along a little way with you, Janey. She wasn't the most joyous — she was a lousy wife.' But even as I said it, I felt regret, loss. She'd been so beautiful ... 'She was cold, she didn't care for anything but money; what she got out of me — a marriage settlement instead of alimony, but it's the same — crippled me in the pocketbook, and she didn't need it. And now that you mention it, it was a woman judge signed the decree. But John Five — if he hired anyone to kill his wife, he could be blackmailed for life. And I don't suppose he likes to spend money and have nothing material to show for it.'

'You can say that again,' Janey said. 'The few times he's used cabs, he asks how much before he puts in the order.' She grinned suddenly. 'Finalizes the order. And he don't tip. But blackmail? The guy that did the murder couldn't blackmail John Five without tipping his own mitt, and that would mean the electric chair. Naw, he'd shut up.'

Lou had brought in a sack of ice cubes and was breaking them up behind the bar using a softball bat. Some of the customers had left. There was now only one man at the bar, but another couple had been added to the ones in the booths. I got up and shoved a quarter in the juke box and punched two Dinah Shore records and a Belafonte that I remembered as being quiet.

When I got back, Janey was frowning. 'It's a matter of finding out which one of the Mt. Hilliard cossacks is suddenly changing his way of life,' she said a little quaintly. 'Buying a new car, maybe getting married, something like that. Sooner or later, my drivers'll find out; they hear everything in town.'

'Sooner or later doesn't do me much good,' I said. 'At any minute old Mr. Gray could cancel my bail. My boss tied the can to me for dragging the company name into this mess. Henry Lighton would pull out if Mr. Gray did.'

'Mr. Gray must think Mac's in this, or he wouldn't be siding with you. Hey, maybe Mac choked her, for John Five!'

I shook my head.

She said: 'Naw,' the light dying from

her eyes. 'He's a cop, that one. No, the old gent sprang you because he and Andy know how Mac is. They wanted to get you out of there before Mac beat you like he did Red.'

It was as simple as that. Of course, Mac must have been in trouble up in the city. He wasn't so old that retirement would be for age; his resignation had been requested. He would never have quit police work till sixty-five forced him to, he was ten years short of that. Andy had suggested that Mr. Gray had bailed me because he wanted to annoy Mac. Henry Lighton had suggested that he'd done it because he thought Mac was slipping, and had made an arrest on me because he was jealous of Andy's interest in me.

This woman thought it was because Mr. Gray was afraid Mac would beat me to death.

One way or another, it seemed fairly certain that Mr. Gray's interest in me had to do with Mac, and not with the murderer. Everyone in Lowndesburg thought so.

But the mystery of Mac and Mr. Gray

was a little one, and it didn't seem to have anything to do with the big one, the only one that mattered — who killed Edith?

Janey said: 'You met any of John Five's Green-and-Tans? He dresses them like forest rangers or tree surgeons, but they're there to guard him, believe you me.' She giggled. 'When I was still in school, a boy I used to go with and me, we thought Mt. Hilllard'd be a nice place for a picnic, like. We were just — It doesn't matter. You met any of the boys?'

'Danny Banion and his partner Crosley. Mac swore them in as special cops.'

'You see what I mean?'

'If John Five knows who killed her, he wouldn't be so scared the murderer would get him.'

Janey half turned her head to the juke box. 'Who put that schmaltz on? John Five ain't completely dumb. He'd want to make noises like he was scared. Danny or Crosley didn't say anything about any of their men quitting?'

I shook my head. 'They wouldn't be likely to chat about Mt. Hilliard affairs to me.'

'Crosley's married,' Janey said. 'Married guys always need more dough. Danny is panting after Andy McLane, a good-looking dish, but a guy'd get Mac for a father-in-law.'

'He's given up panting, as you put it. He's going back into the Forest Service, whether she'll go with him or not.'

Janey snapped her head up. She looked at me, her eyes bright. 'You got it!'

I looked behind me. I looked at my hands to see if symptoms of a disease had broken out. 'I have what?'

'There's no money in the Forest Service,' Janey said. 'When I was in college I went with some boys in the forestry school. They said you almost had to have a private income to make out in the U.S. service,'

I was staring at her.

'Danny quit the Service to work for John Five. Now he's quitting John Five to go back. So he's come into some dough.'

Like an idiot, I said, 'Where did you go to college?'

'State. I was a sorority girl, too, and I don't blow my nose in my fingers; they taught me better. Wake up, mush-head. We got your murderer, Danny Banion. John Five paid him enough to do it for Danny to live in the tall timber the rest of his life, making eyes at the trees.'

'Banion seems too much of a Boy Scout for that sort of thing.'

Janey began laughing. I guess I looked interested, because she said, 'When I was thirteen my kid brother joined the Scouts. When they met at our house, the patrol leader used to put the other kids to tying knots while he and I went out in the pantry. He was fifteen.'

'You ought to write your memoirs, Janey. You've got the experience, and you've got the imagination. That stuff about Banion is pure moonshine.'

She looked at me, the dark eyes like buttons. 'You don't want to get loose,' she said. 'Not if it means talking mean to somebody. You want to go to the chair like a little gentleman, with your chin in the air and a stiff upper lip. You ought to be in the funny papers, mister.' She got up and stamped, high-heeled and hard-heeled, to the bar, and sat down on a stool, her legs very pretty, and started talking to Lou. I scooped up my change and went after her.

Janey was saying: 'The Dodgers ought to be hot as a homemade pistol this year . . . '

I went out. She'd given me plenty to think of; but Danny Banion? It seemed impossible, even if she and the patrol leader had played games in the pantry. Maybe Danny had been a Woodland Ranger instead of a Boy Scout.

8

Spring was still in the process of avoiding Lowndesburg. I couldn't blame it; I wished I'd done the same. Everyone in this little town wanted me to do something for any reason in the world but one associated with my own best interests.

I got in my car, eyes down, frowning, and Lieutenant Gamble said: 'If you drink, don't drive.' He was sitting next to the driver's seat, relaxed.

'If you drive, don't drink,' I said, completing the safety council slogan. 'I won't ask how you found me; it couldn't have been hard.'

'It wasn't,' Gamble said. 'My boys are watching all the roads, so you didn't leave town, and a Keystone Cop could find a car parked in a town this size.'

'I suppose if I start the motor, I get pinched for drunk driving.'

'I'm only a lieutenant; we leave

important cases like that to the captains and inspectors. I wanted to talk to you, and this is as good a place as any other.'

'Talk is turning my hair gray. And all of it for my own good, till I take a second look.'

'Oh?'

'A lady named Janey Dandler. A taxi driver, or something like that. She wants me to make a big false arrest case because McLane punctured her boyfriend's kidney.'

Lieutenant Gamble nodded his square-cut head. 'Give me the dope and I'll be glad to check it out for you.'

'Why do you people say 'check out' instead of just 'check'? Anyway, it's probably true.'

The lieutenant unbuttoned his coat, took a notebook out of his inner-suit pocket, a pencil from somewhere, and got ready to write. 'Mr. Porter, never take anything for the truth that you haven't checked out — checked, I'm sorry — yourself, to the best of your ability.'

'It can't leave you much time for your regular meals,' I said. 'All right. Miss Jane

Dandler told me she was engaged to a man named Red, who drove a hack for her father's company.'

'Red?'

'She also told me, and he confirmed it, that said Red was the brother of a man named Lou who owns the bistro I just left. His name would be on the liquor license.'

'Red told you this?'

'Red wasn't there. Lou . . . ' I went on with the story. Gamble took it down in shorthand; of course he would know shorthand, as he would know fingerprinting, photography and any other simple arts likely to be of aid to the good state trooper.

I didn't discuss Janey's suspicions about John Five and Danny Banion. Not because I wanted to keep them to myself, but because I thought Lieutenant Gamble would laugh at me for even listening to that kind of story, not to mention paying for the drinks while I heard it.

When I finished, he stowed the notebook away and said, 'That shouldn't be hard to verify or disprove, as the case may be.'

'Part of it you'd know offhand. Does Mac have a reputation for brutality?'

His chiseled lips closed and he said nothing. It was as eloquent a nothing as you'd want to hear, if anybody ever wanted to hear an eloquent nothing.

'All cops are good, eh? All outsiders stay outside.'

'Something like that. Now, as I said, I wanted to talk to you. About Edith Hilliard. Edith Stayne Porter Hilliard.'

'How about the notebook, copper? How about the speech that anything I say can be used against me?'

Lieutenant Gamble sighed a patient sigh. He unbuttoned his coat again. 'The notebook, certainly, if you don't mind. The other — that's England, not the United States. Or maybe it isn't even England, but just English detective novels.'

We both sat. Finally the lieutenant sighed again. 'What are you waiting for?'

'For you to ask questions.'

He shook his head. 'On second

thought, maybe you ought to drive away from here. I'm not unknown, and if Miss Dangler saw you with me, it might dam up any future information she was disposed to give you.'

I started the motor. As the car pulled out of the parking lot, I said, 'That's beneath you, Lieutenant Gamble. Attempting to disarm me by being less than a superman. Dandler, not Dangler.'

He almost grinned. He stopped it when it was nothing more than a controlled smile, but he almost grinned. 'All right, Dandler. Where did you meet your ex-wife, Mr. Porter?'

So I told him. In '53 I was assistant personnel manager for a factory in Milwaukee, and she came to work as a stenographer. 'She didn't stay in the pool long, of course. My boss snared her for a private secretary. So I saw a lot of her, and — '

A car passed us, going very fast, almost going into the curb on the left to get by us. As it went ahead, it made a sirenish noise. There was lettering on the side, J. F. Gray's — Mac's car.

I said: 'Follow that car, bud?'

Deadpan, Lieutenant Gamble said: 'Follow the heap, chief.' Then he laughed. 'Only slower. I set some store on my life. And keep on talking.'

'The assistant personnel manager sees a lot of the personnel manager's secretary. On the fourth date, I asked her to marry me.'

Ahead, Mac's siren was now in full cry. Considering Mac, it should have bayed like a foxhound, but it sounded just like a police siren.

Lieutenant Gamble said: 'I see. So you didn't know her too well. You were in personnel. So you had access to the files, of course. Where did she work before, where did her first husband work, who were her parents, her maiden name? I suppose you can give me all that.'

I looked at him, startled.

He flipped a thumb forward. 'The road, the road.'

I looked at the road. 'I don't ask a woman for references before I fall in love with her. I don't know anybody who does, or didn't before I met you. Who was your wife's maternal grandfather?'

'Why, he was a storekeeper, postmaster and justice of the peace in Iowa,' Lieutenant Gamble said, 'though he was born in Canajoharie, New York. His family took him to Iowa when he was six. They had a farm there, but when he was thirteen he took to clerking in the local general store and — '

I yelled, 'All right, all right. So you're perfect. I'm not. I don't know a damn thing about Edith except that she was beautiful, and I made the common male mistake of thinking that beauty connotes warmth, elegance of soul, intelligence and everything else that's nice, including sugar and spice.'

'You don't even know who Stayne was?'

Ahead, a knot of cars were stopped. One of them had a red blinker on the roof. I said, 'I guess Mac's run the fox to earth,' and began to slow down. 'Why, Mr. Stayne was Edith's father, I presume.'

'Nan for negative,' Lieutenant Gamble said. 'She gave a date and a place of birth on her driver's license. No such birth is recorded in Canton, Ohio. We've sent out to Nevada for her marriage license. If she gave the same date and birthplace there, it can be presumed that Stayne was a name from a previous marriage.'

The knot of cars resolved itself into two private sedans, one with smashed headlights and radiator, the other with a smashed-in side; and Mac's car and a state trooper's cruiser. I stopped and looked at Lieutenant Gamble. A tall man in a trooper's uniform came over to us.

I said: 'She could have changed her name.'

'That would presume a criminal past,' Lieutenant Gamble said, 'and therefore that her fingerprints were on file with the FBI, which they aren't.' He touched his forehead in answer to the trooper's salute. 'Yes, Roush?'

'We're a quarter of a mile inside Lowndesburg limits, sir,' Roush said. 'I'm letting the chief handle it.'

'Right. You can resume patrol.'

'Sir.' Trooper Roush saluted and started away.

I said 'Wait a minute,' and Roush

turned back, looked inquiringly at the lieutenant. 'Lieutenant Gamble, you're slipping. How do you know this man is a state officer? He could have knocked off Trooper Roush, stolen his badge, car and uniform, and made up his face to resemble the victim. Hadn't you better take his fingerprints, compare his dental work?'

Lieutenant Gamble said: 'Resume patrol, Roush. Mr. Porter's a humorist.'

Roush said 'Yes, sir,' in a tone that sounded as if he didn't agree about me. He went to his car and started it before he'd taken the microphone out of his hand.

'Look, papa, no hands,' I said. 'Hey, I've got an idea. Edith changed her name from Stein to Stayne to avoid prejudice.' Ahead of us, Mac was busy with his notebook.

'Was she Jewish?'

'No. But now that we've stopped kidding around, she could have lied about her age.'

Lieutenant Gamble nodded as though I'd said something wise. We both watched

Otto McLane start to pace off skidmarks. The lieutenant said: 'Well, I thought of that. But the city directories for ten years back of the birthdate she gave show no one named Stayne. Or Stein. I thought of that, too.'

'What don't you think of?'

Lieutenant Gamble snorted. 'I don't think much of District Attorney Norton Prince for letting Henry Lighton get bail set on you. I'd like to see you in a cell. I would indeed.'

'My pal.'

He shrugged. 'Call it my passion for neatness, Mr. Porter. I like all my clues neatly filed away, including suspects. Let's get out and listen to Chief McLane handle this case. It might be instructive.'

Outside the car, it was not just a cool spring; it was a returned winter. I sneezed once, and Mac turned his head from his notebook, saw me, frowned and then saw Lieutenant Gamble and shrugged. He turned back to the drivers of the two cars, who were standing there as though they had been caught stealing sheep.

'All right,' Mac said. 'You can drive

into Lowndesburg if your cars will go. Mr. Snider, I'm sure yours will. It's just a smashed door and some dents.'

'About two hundred dollars,' Snider said.

'Your own fault.'

'I hit him with my side? You're crazy.'

'You were going too fast. You saw Mr. Winfrey's car coming around that curve. You stepped on the brakes, and skidded right into his path.'

'Have a heart, Officer! My insurance — '

Mac said, slowly, 'It's against the law to drive in this state without insurance. What were you going to say?'

Snider looked around at all of us. He shrugged and got into his battered car, and started it after a little trouble. The vehicle moved down the road towards Lowndesburg slowly and crankily, like a crab who has decided to go straight.

Mac said, 'I gotta get this road clear. Try your car, Mr. Winfrey.'

Mr. Winfrey smelled of money. So did his car, a Lincoln four-door. But you can't tell, these days of easy credit. 'She oughtn't to be driven that way,' he said. 'The motor will overheat. Send me a tow car, Officer.'

Mac said, 'I like my streets clean. The weather bureau says there's a storm coming in; I want this heap off the road.'

'Listen, my good man — '

Mac's voice was a Boston bull's bark: 'I'm not your good man. I'm police chief of this town. And let me tell you . . . '

Lieutenant Gamble had my elbow and was leading me away. The firm features of the lieutenant were drooping.

He got in beside me, and I started my car. I was headed back to town before I said anything, and then all I said was, 'So?'

Lieutenant Gamble shrugged. 'It didn't mean anything. Every cop has his off days, his off hours. It was cold out there, and that Winfrey was wearing an overcoat worth more than Mac makes in a month.'

I stopped for a fixed sign, where the town really began. 'You believe what you're saying, Lieutenant?'

His hand clenched and beat his knee. 'I believe nothing till I've checked it — out.

I'll make inquiries up in the city.'

'What can you do? This is a democracy. The people of Lowndesburg can elect any police chief they want to.'

He looked at me almost with affection. 'I wish I had had your nice soft background. You really believe that, don't you?'

'Who's to stop them?' But I sensed it was a naive question.

'Why, I am. It's a democracy, sure, but with only two parties. If the state police go to the bosses of those two parties and say they can't work with a local officer or a district attorney, he doesn't get nominated.'

I pulled the car over to the curb and parked carefully. Mac would be coming back in a minute, and I didn't want a ticket; and Mac would give me one, even though I was with a state police officer, if I parked an inch out of line.

'Your theory isn't working too well,' I said. 'How about Norton Prince?'

Lieutenant Gamble was in his frank mood. I was innocent — no, nice and soft were what he had called me — but I was

162

dimly aware that he was most dangerous when he appeared most frank.

He said: 'Norton Prince does all right with the other Lowndes County lawyers against him. He's as good as we could ask. No one who would take the job is good enough for Henry Lighton, though.'

'So you think I'll get off.' I didn't make a question of it. Mac's car went by us then, back into Lowndesburg. Mac had not looked at us when he went out, nor now returning; and he had given us only that one brief glance at the scene of the accident. Yet I was sure Mac didn't miss much.

Lieutenant Gamble said: 'I'm only sure of one thing. And that is, when I get up on that stand in the courtroom, I'm not going to be asked why I didn't know this, that or the other thing about the case I was supposed to prepare. And so, my friend, I check everything.'

'Out.'

He didn't smile. 'Sooner or later, I'm going to find out who Edith Stayne was. I think you know. If you do, tell me now.' Any shade of friendliness was gone.

I said, 'I really don't know.'

'Got a copy of your marriage certificate, your notification of divorce?'

'I never had the first. The other's in a tin box in my bureau, in my apartment in Chicago.'

'The Chicago cops will send it to me. All right. Drive me downtown, the courthouse square.'

I drove him there and let him out. He didn't say goodbye to me, or thanks, or anything else. He was, for the moment, through with me.

9

Now I didn't have any place to go. Lou's bar was impossible, with Lou and Janey staring at me, urging me to go do something I didn't know how to do.

The hotel would be full of newspaper-men unless I stayed in my room, which was like locking myself in a cell. Cell, I could go to the courthouse and get one-armed Knowles to let me in, and we could chat. I could —

People were coming across the square towards my car. I'd been spotted. I had to go someplace. I started the car for that place, not knowing where it would be, not caring, just getting away.

It turned out, of course, to be Andy's house. Mac's house. Mr. Gray's house, really.

I had a nice, soft background, like Lieutenant Gamble had said. I needed a woman's shoulder to lean on. Andy's.

There was a driveway winding around

a gnarled old tree to one side of the house. I followed it and parked my car in the back yard, behind the house, where I hoped it couldn't be seen from the street.

As I stepped out, I sneezed twice. The change in the weather, the dragging fatigue of all the excitement, the grinding fear I carried were using me up. I was going to have a cold.

Not a serious thing, a cold in the head. Just fatal was all — to a man who had to use that head to stay alive. I didn't know whether I was that man or not.

Cars passed out in the street, and I waited till their noise faded before going back to the front door. But a noise at the back of the house attracted me.

Old Man Gray was rapping on one of the conservatory windows with his cane. I went in to him. He looked at me and said, 'Something the cat dragged in,' and raised his cackling voice. 'Andy!'

A door closed in the front of the house and high heels clicked towards us. Then Andy came into the conservatory, closing the door behind her. She said: 'Yes, Grandpa?' and then she saw me; and before I knew it, we were hanging on to each other, and I felt that I had come home.

Then she was crying on my shoulder, and I was patting her. 'I didn't know where you were,' she said over and over again. 'I was so worried.' She'd had time to think over my kiss, and she'd made up her mind the right way. Or, I worried, maybe she was just sorry for me . . .

She broke away and sat down in the chair nearest the one her grandfather usually used. 'Gramps,' she said, 'tell me to stop making an idiot of myself.'

The old man sat down in his own chair and shook his head. He'd dropped the role of cackling old gadfly.

'No,' he said. 'You're doin' right, Andy. You got a heart, an' you're doin' just right to show it. Not enough heart in this damned old world, as it is. You love the woman, Paul?'

I said, 'I never knew what love was like till I met her.'

'You want to marry her?'

Andy said 'Hey,' but I just gave her a look and grinned and said, 'Of course.'

'Been waiting for this day,' he said. He got his shawl and wrapped it around his shoulders. 'I liked you from the time you sat here last night and wouldn't let me rile you. You're my kind of man, young fella, and I don't mind sayin' it. Not a bit.'

I sneezed. He pulled back from me. 'Don't do that,' he said. 'One good cold would kill me. You takin' anything for that sneeze?'

I shook my head.

'Vitamin C,' he said. He was getting his cackle back again. 'That's what the doc gives me if I sneeze. Fifteen hundred units of Vitamin C. Get him some, Andy.'

'It's all out. I gave you the last of it Thursday.'

'Well, g'wan downtown an' git him some. Don't just sit there!'

'I'll go get it myself,' I said. 'I'm not a baby, Mr. Gray.'

'No, but you're a ring-tailed celebrity,' he said. 'The gal in the drugstore would plain faint away with ecstasy at the privilege of takin' your money, touching the famous hand that did or did not strangle Edith Hilliard. You stay here. On your horse, Andy.'

If Mac had gone a little nuts, I could see why. Living with the old gent — especially living on his bounty — wouldn't be easy. I tried to make a pun of mutiny and bounty, failed, and accepted a glass of sherry from Andy. Mr. Gray already had his, and was looking at it with the passion of a Tarquin for Lucretia.

Andy knew her grandfather; she was hurrying away. I heard the front door slam and the car start.

Mr. Gray took a sip of his wine and said, 'Where have you been, Paul? Had to get Andy out of the way; if things are goin' agin you, she'd whoop and holler. Report, youngster; how's it going?'

'I've been consorting with light ladies, or a reasonable facsimile of one,' I said. 'The queen of local hacky circles has been spilling the dope on Otto McLane.'

He said, 'Do tell,' which he had probably picked upon a radio program thirty years before.

I told.

He nodded when I finished. 'Got to do something about Otto,' he said. 'He's gettin' queer an' queerer.'

'Lieutenant Gamble's going to look into his record.'

Mr. Gray shook his head. 'Nope. Nothin' there. It's my fault. He was all right while he was up in the city. 'Twas me corrupted him, with my money, such as it is. Chance to draw his pension, *and* the income from the business, too.'

I shook my head. 'If a man's a louse, it's his own fault, not the fault of the innocent friend who unwittingly places him in ideal louse country.'

The cackle was clear and unfeigned. 'Got to remember that. Got to tell that to Andy. You been talking with Lieutenant Gamble, too.'

I nodded, any joy dying in my heart. 'That I have.'

'And — ' The old eyes bored into me from above the sherry glass.

I looked out at the darkening, lowering day. Little flakes of snow were coming down, mixed with the drizzle. 'He still thinks I did it. He can't find any trace of anyone else, and he's conceited enough to believe if there was anyone else, he'd find him. So all he's doing now is tying up loose ends. He's trying to dig up a third husband for Edith, one before me, and find out where he was.' I shook my head. 'Two ex-husbands in this little town on one day. I don't expect it.'

'But they got no witness you killed her?' I shook my head. 'Then, boy, you'll probably be all right. That Henry Lighton eats circumstantial evidence like it was lady-fingers.' He cackled. 'Hope I'm well enough to go to the trial. It'll be a lolla — '

The phone rang before he finished the giant, long, old-fashioned word. He put his hands on the arms of his chair and started to rise. I reached forward to help him, and he waved me away with a thrust of his bony, wattled chin.

The phone had rung four times before he got to it. You would think they would have gotten a long cord, so he could have it near him, but maybe he didn't like phones.

He said: 'Yes, who? Why, Hank, you old

— He what . . . ? By God, I'll — What do you think, Hank? Yeah, I know you're not a lawyer, but you hung around there long enough to — Ten days, huh? Well, by God, ten days from now you'll hear me down there, blastin' the calcimine off the walls.'

He slammed the phone back in its cradle, turned and stared at me, began to shake a long finger in the air. 'I was sayin' I had to do something about Otto! Well, he's done something about me! That was Hank deVries, down at the courthouse. Otto's gotten the judge to write out a paper I'm senile!'

Whatever was left in the old man — a pint of blood, a pound of muscles, a little marrow in his chalky bones — was shaking him unbearably. I stepped forward, grabbed him, tried to get him to sit down. But my touch made him shake worse, and I let go again.

I said: 'That can't be done. There has to be a hearing, doctors have to examine you, you've got the right . . . '

His mouth was moving, as though he wanted to spit, but couldn't get up the moisture. 'Injunction,' he said thickly. 'Otto and I — partners. Enjoin me against spendin' my money — any money — own money — '

He staggered across the sunporch and tore at a picture on the house wall. It came down. He dropped it, shattering the glass, tearing the steel engraving of a paddlewheel steamer.

'Bond,' he said. 'Cancel your bail-bond.'

'Mr. Gray, sit down. Andy'll be back in a minute, we'll talk this over . . . '

'No time,' he said. Two bricks came out of the wall and dropped on top of the picture. There was the dial of a safe there. The bony claws spun the dial. 'Henry Lighton will drop,' he said. 'Drop you.' Color, not good red, but a murky purple was staining the old cheeks. There wasn't anything I could do; restraining him would only increase his rage.

The safe came open, and there was a sheaf of green in his hands. He thrust it out at me. 'Take it to Lighton,' his thick voice said. 'Keep him on your side. Two thousand, been here for years.'

And, by God, it had. The bills were the old, big ones that I hardly remembered ever seeing. I'd gotten them for birthdays when I was a very little boy.

But old Mr. Gray was shoving the money at me. Two thousand dollars; it would not keep me out on bail, but it would free Henry Lighton to try and spring me some other way. I reached for it.

Mr. Gray's hands came open, and the money fell, as things fall in a nightmare just as you're going to touch them. Foolishly, I speared at the falling leaves like a puppy after a butterfly.

But then the money was forgotten. For the purple began to drain out of Mr. Gray's face, and he bent forward, clutched at his chest, his knees buckled, and he fell, though I tried to catch him. He landed on the scattered money, but two thousand dollars, even in big notes, is no cushion. I dropped to my knees and felt for his pulse. It was there, all right; it fluttered for four or five beats and then was still.

And so was he. There'd been so little

life in him that he started chilling at once.

I knelt there, staring at him.

Outside, a car came up; for a moment I thought it was Andy, and was thankful. But the steps that came back towards me were hard and firm and masculine. Mac or Lieutenant Gamble or one of the special forester-cops, coming to pick me up; my bail was canceled.

I started to rake the money together, to take it or send it to Henry Lighton. Which was a stupid waste of time. Now I realized how it looked: Mr. Gray dead, money on the floor, the safe open, the picture broken.

I had no right to the money; the injunction would cover it, too. And no one in his right mind could look at the scene and see anything but a guilty man — me — gathering this loot. A desperate, guilty man who had undoubtedly killed Mr. Gray; maybe not purposely, but in the course of using violence to get him to open the safe.

Probably I didn't think all that just then; not in words, anyway. If I did, I was a mighty quick thinker, because in the time it took those hard footsteps to bang from the front door to the sunporch-conservatory, I was out the same glass door I'd come in through, out and in the back yard and behind the gnarled, leafless fruit tree there.

10

Any fear I had felt up to now was kid sniff, nursery-grade fear. Now I was really alone, and on the run, and from something real. Maybe I hadn't believed they could get me for killing Edith, when I hadn't even been there; maybe, though I'd had some pretty bad moments in Mac's jail and in the hotel room with Gamble.

But I believed with all my quaking heart, with all my feeble brain, that I could be arrested, tried and convicted for the murder of Mr. Gray. I'd been there, only too obviously; my fingerprints were all over the place. They could hang a motive on me; they could say I had flown into a rage when Mr. Gray told me my bail-bond was cancelled, had threatened him, and so he had gone to the safe; and since being threatened isn't good for sick men of eighty, he had dropped dead.

Maybe it wasn't murder. Maybe just

manslaughter or homicide, or whatever they called the crime that put you in prison from twenty years to life. But with this against me, who'd help me with the charge of murder, the charge of murdering of Edith? Not Henry Lighton, who loved money and hated the penniless. Not Andy, who had loved her grandfather. Not . . .

I forgot all that in the howling misery of knowing I had now lost Andy for good.

It was colder out than it had been yesterday. I had no overcoat. I shivered a little, and kept moving away from the house.

This was a back yard, a very big one. There was a ruined tennis court and a building that had been a stable once, but was now locked up and dirty-windowed. I could hide there. It was obvious I couldn't use my car; the man who had been on his way was now surely in the conservatory and would see me.

The man — I had to find out who that man was.

So I turned back for the house. First I looked around. Nobody could see into this yard; no other houses overlooked it. If they had, it would have been dangerous to do what I did, which was crouch down like a kid playing cowboy and creep up on the conservatory bent over, making myself inconspicuous.

The panes of glass behind the plants were clean. I could see into the room clearly. Three people in there: Mac, Lieutenant Gamble and Henry Lighton. They were bending over Mr. Gray — over Mr. Gray's body.

I had to get going — on foot, of course — and quickly, before another sneezing fit told them I was there. I remembered the medicine Mr. Gray had sent Andy for and wished I had it, but it was time to leave. Where did I go from here? I wasn't quite sure, but there were two things I had to do: find a place to hide, and find Edith's murderer.

The latter seemed an impossible task. I didn't know a half dozen people in Lowndesburg and the valley, except policemen — I knew plenty of those. And since that seemed an unlikely field to plough, who else was there for me to suspect? The sensible thing to do was go back into the conservatory and talk to Henry Lighton. Even now he might — just might — be telling the lieutenant things in my favor. But I started moving towards the back of the yard. I went around the old stable; there was an alley there, unpaved. A woven wire fence had separated the yard from the alley, but it had broken down; some of it had, in fact, broken up, carried from the ground by growing shrubs and little trees.

The country was taking Lowndesburg back, as a jungle takes over an abandoned village. But this wasn't the jungle; it was the midwest of the United States, the great Mississippi Valley.

Still, Lowndesburg was dying. With its part-time police chief and its one-armed jailer, with its battered hotel and its amateur farmers — one a semi-retired lawyer, one a distiller of apple brandy — Lowndesburg was dying. It might be reborn as a suburb — exurb was probably a better word — as superhighways, reaching out for it from the city, made commutation possible. But it was going dead for the time being.

And, dying, it had reached out and killed me, too.

Then, suddenly, I knew whom I had to see. John Five. John Hilliard V, the master of Mt. Hilliard, the man who married Edith after she had left me. The master of Mt. Hilliard, the master of Lowndesburg, the master of all Lowndes County.

The state police could be firmly, impartially efficient; little Mac would bark and snap and growl; Henry Lighton could be learned and nationally known; but John Hilliard the Fifth, John Five, had the money, and money talked in a universal language.

Janey Dandler had claimed John Five had killed Edith, or had Danny Banion do it, but this was too silly for words. And yet, it might be possible, but I'd need more than Janey's scraps of hearsay and bolts of hatred to sew it up. Still, I had better use Janey's idea. The time had come for me to use anything and everything I could lay my hands on. My hands and my feeble, sneezing brain.

To the sneezes, the wheezes and the

running nose, a cough was now being added.

I looked around me. I surveyed the situation. Then I sneezed again.

Doctors will assure you that a head cold is seldom, *per se*, fatal. But I was about to be killed by one; this one was keeping me from thinking, just when thinking was the only thing that might keep me from the electric chair.

Full of self-pity, I kept walking.

Mt. Hilliard was about six miles out of town, a short jaunt in a car, a long walk for a man who was being hunted by all the police in the world.

Fortunately, the Gray house was on the edge of town. It was on the north edge, and Mt. Hilliard rose above the east road, but at least I was in a sparsely populated area. I headed uphill, going further north than the Gray place. Here the houses were far apart, a house to an acre or an acre and a half; almost small farms. A lot of the places were deserted, their windows broken, their porches falling down. On one big lot there was nothing left but a square hole in the ground and a chimney rising high; I could see where there had been a fireplace on each side of the chimney.

I kept on climbing.

The paving ran out, the houses got scarcer. Fields along here were sloping and they were going back into forest; second growth spruce and pine and hardwood were pushing in.

Rain began to fall again, and it got a lot colder, almost too cold for rain, before I saw what I wanted: a house with telephone wires leading in, no observant neighbors, and no signs of life.

The last took checking. The garage was open and empty and no smoke came from the chimneys; but I was cautious approaching. I peered in all the downstairs windows before I tried the front door. Of course, it was locked.

Hope springs eternal in the heart of a fool. I fiddled around with my keyring, trying my car keys, the key to the office, to the apartment in Chicago, some keys I'd forgotten the use of, but none of them worked. I tried a gas company credit card, like it says in the detective stories, but either I didn't know how to use it or this door had never read detective stories.

Then I tried windows, but whoever lived up here in the woods was a careful householder; the windows were locked. Finally I tried the back door; it was open. I walked in. But I was still cautious; I prowled the ground floor before I sat down at the phone. No signs anyone had been here for hours.

There were three taxi companies, none of them named Dandler: Checker, Yellow, and Lowndesburg. There was a private number for a Horace Dandler, and another for H. J. Dandler, Jr. I tried the first one; no answer. The second would probably be the husband of the sister-in-law who was the other dispatcher.

I didn't want to talk to anyone I didn't have to. I tried Yellow, and when a man answered, I hung up; then I tried Lowndesburg, and Janey said: 'Taxi,' and I said: 'Have to talk to you, Janey.'

She was a smart one; or maybe she'd been thinking of me. She said: 'Where?'

'About four miles past Mr. Gray's house, on the road that goes uphill and then turns toward Mt. Hilliard.'

'Brown house with green trim? Two-story?'

'Yes.'

'McAllister's,' she said. 'They'll be home in an hour or so. Wait in the first bunch of pine trees away from town.'

'Okay, Janey.'

'I'll be a little while.'

I hung up. I'd made two phone calls; I shoved a quarter into the lining of an overstuffed chair, looked around to be sure I hadn't left anything — though I hadn't much to leave — and went out the back door, eyeing the ice box as I went by. Eating was a half-remembered habit.

The road was clay, slippery, and inclined to ball on the feet. I stumbled on, and then pines were dark on either side of me. Leafy trees were still in bud, and liable to lose these if this frost got any worse. The pines were rough-barked, but their needles made dry standing and they kept the drizzle dripping in predictable places. I found a dry place to lean and lighted a cigarette.

That cigarette was out and another one

was started before a car pulled into the pine grove, stopped, and Janey got out. There was a man at the wheel of the car, and I nearly turned and ran when I saw him; I had been sure she'd come alone.

She said, 'What are you doing up here?'

'Waiting for you. I've got to see John Five; maybe you can figure a way to help me.' But I was looking over her shoulder at the car.

'That's my brother,' she said. 'And he's got a gun pointed at you.'

'I didn't kill Mr. Gray. McLane got an injunction out, claiming the old gentleman was senile; it killed him.'

She said, 'It sounds like Mac,' and then was silent a minute. Then she said, 'Got a cigarette? I forgot to bring any. Had to get my sister-in-law to watch the switchboard; she'll probably smoke them all up.'

My hands were shaking, so she had to take the package from me and light her own smoke.

'Mac,' I said, 'he's as bad as you said.' Mac was the key to this woman.

'The old man was good to him. How the hell can I get you to see John Five?'

186

That was a question beyond my abilities. I stood there, shivering in the cold and wet, and said, 'You know everything that goes on. How do I get through the Green-and-Tan?'

She shook her head, frowning. 'Danny Banion's on night duty, or it would be a cinch. He's a sucker for women. But Crosley . . . Lemme talk to my brother.'

She went back down to the cab. Brother, whatever his name was, climbed out, a service .45 big in his hand, and they stood talking, the automatic pointed at the ground; but Janey stood with her back to me, so the brother could keep an eye on my dangerous face. Then she turned and waved a hand at me, and I went down, too.

'Get in the cab.'

Dear brother added: 'Keep your hands in your pockets. I don't want your fingerprints all over the heap.'

'My fingerprints have frozen and fallen off.'

'Very funny.'

He got in the driver's seat, and Janey and I got in the back. She was eyeing me with less of a frown, but she looked worried. 'You're freezing to death.'

I said that death would be a pleasant relief from the way I felt.

'It's colder up here than it is in town. Wetter, too. This weather will break; we get it every spring.'

She had a woolen muffler around her neck. She unwound it and handed it to me. It did some good. But my teeth kept on chattering, and she reached over, pulled me down on her shoulder, and put her arm around me. That did a lot more good, but she was as impersonal as a veterinarian. Brother pulled over to the side of the road, stopped the car, said: 'Here.'

We got out. He U-turned the car and was gone.

'He'll wait around the next bend for me,' Janey said. 'He never liked Red to begin with.'

There wasn't anything I could say to that. I changed the subject. 'Isn't he worried about his tire tracks?'

'We get our tires from Monkey Ward or Sears and Roebuck. So do half the other people in town. No sweat on that one.'

Ahead of us a dirt road crossed the one we were on, which had been paved once and then gone back to dirt. A sign said that trespassers would be prosecuted by the Hilliard Land & Improvement Company. I couldn't see any improvements, but the crossing road looked queer. I went and put my hand on it. It was springy; John Five had hauled tan bark up here for his bridle path.

'Twenty miles long,' Janey said. 'All landscaped, all paved so his horsey-worsies won't hurt their feet.'

'Their footums,' I said.

'Shut up,' she said. 'My brother said the guard was due to ride by here any minute, and horses don't make any noise on that stuff.'

'That how you got caught when you were in high school?'

'Yeah.' She giggled a little, though we were both talking in whispers.

'What were you doing?'

'Shut up,' she said again. 'Start downhill. I'll keep the Green-and-Tan here for about twenty minutes, one way or another.'

'Or another,' I said.

'Depends on which one it is. Good luck. You'll see Mt. Hilliard in about twenty minutes, if you keep walking downhill. It's up to you.'

The bark was soft and comforting under my feet. I stopped once and dug down; it was a foot deep, at least. Twenty miles of it must have cost John Five a small fortune. I began coughing again; I couldn't sneak up on anyone that way.

There was a very nice tulip tree overhanging the bridle path. I rested under it, lighted a cigarette and tried to figure how many ten-ton truckloads of bark had been hauled up here. The cigarette, perversely, stopped the cough.

I was facing the valley, but not much of it could be seen. John Five's dendrologists, helping nature, had planted trees that kept an equestrian from being bothered by a view of the machine age that had developed below. An occasional roof could be seen, a patch of cement highway catching the patchy sun; nothing more.

I put out the cigarette and started walking.

The wrong time was on my wristwatch when I got to Mt. Hilliard. Understandably. I had not wound it the night before. But the hunger in my belly, the ache in my legs, the watery light in my eyes all told me I had used up the morning and part of the afternoon.

The bridle path ended in the woods, with stables and white-fenced corrals, or paddocks, or whatever they were called at Mt. Hilliard. This plant was set down in the woods, on a lower level than the house and the garage; broad, gentle steps led from one to the other.

There were men working around the stables, several of them, leading horses in fancy overcoats around, and polishing leather. Two men were busy putting new shoes on a long-legged red animal who didn't seem to be appreciating the honor. As I watched from the woods, he kicked out — though one man was holding his hoof up on a knee, another was holding his head — and the man at the hoof end swore. He let go of the hoof and stood up, shaking his hand, which had turned bright red.

Everybody around came to inspect the wound, and I used the opportunity to work halfway around the ledge and get to the stairs going up to the house. But I didn't use the stairs. I went up the steep slope of the woods alongside, using the trees and shrubs for cover, moving cautiously. Hungry and dog-tired, I lost my breath quickly. I sat down under a little moose maple and looked back down.

I'd come higher and further than I thought. The stables were dwarfed, now; the big red horse was only a toy. Sunlight played on the scene, and the man with the ripped hand now had a bright white bandage around his palm. It looked like a Currier and Ives print, and gave the impression of an age, an innocence that I doubted had ever really existed. A man could feel like a god, coming down this hill and seeing that layout below him and knowing he had made it and owned it.

I hurried up the hill to meet that man. My journey ended near the back door and the big garage. Yesterday had been Thursday, and the servants were all off; today was Friday and they were hard at work, proving to their master that a day's pleasure had not ruined them for his devoted service. Two chauffeurs were out polishing cars; a gardener was covering shrubs with gunnysacks and tying them down against the winter. A maid came to the back door and put a load of trash into a can.

I hadn't a prayer in the world of getting across that service yard to the house. I'd seen six or eight men down at the stables, three up here. No doubt there were enough women servants in the house to overpower me by sheer numbers. And the Green-and-Tans would be on call, with riot guns.

I picked another tree — a black walnut — and rested under it. I couldn't smoke here, or John Five's fire department would start blowing off sirens.

Edith had certainly fallen into it. As I thought back, our arguments over

193

whether we could afford to eat dinner at a restaurant three times in one week were a little silly. If she and John Five had had arguments like that, it would have been as to whether it was entirely sensible to buy more than three restaurants in any one week, the bookkeeping being what it was.

When I had been married to her, she had made me almost angry enough to kill her, if I'd been built that way. And all my vaporous reflections boiled down to the thought that John Five had felt the same way, and maybe had been built that way. A big maybe.

But would she have bedeviled a man with all this money? Not if he was generous. And John Five looked mighty generous to what was his: his horses, his cars, his trees, his shrubs and his house. Surely his wife would have had all the conspicuous expenditure her cold heart could desire.

'She wouldn't irk him,' I told the black walnut. 'She wouldn't irk him.' And on that quaint line, I fell asleep.

11

I know it sounds unbelievable: that a man in my position, hunted, harassed, in imminent danger of losing life, limb and liberty would choose that particular time, that particular piece of hostile territory, to take a nap in. Since then I've asked a couple of doctors about it; one of them had the answer. He said it hadn't been physical exhaustion that made me cork off, but mental retreat: the human brain can face just so much frustration, just so much despair, and then it quits; it needs a rest.

At any rate, I didn't feel rested when I woke up. I was stiff and miserable with cold. My neck felt as though any sudden movement would snap it like an icicle. Both my wrists were numb and sore, as though I'd kept my fists clenched all the time I slept; and my back ached.

It was not quite dark yet, but there were lights on in the house. The chauffeurs had put the cars away; now one of them came out and went down the line of drive-out doors, testing the locks. Then he went back into the house. People kept passing in front of the kitchen windows, which presently began to fog over.

I got my feet under me and stood up, rubbing the back of my neck, twisting my shoulders and hips to get my circulation going.

Not knowing the inside of Mt. Hilliard, how could I plan? The master would be in the front part of the house, having a cocktail or sherry while his faithful army prepared his dinner.

Or the master would be upstairs, having a bath, a nap, or a massage.

Or the master would be in the attic, chasing bats.

How could I tell?

It was getting dark enough to do a little scouting. With luck I might see John Five through a window. I'd know him: he would be eight feet tall and made of solid gold.

I moved downhill over the crisp grass.

From the feel of the air, there might be a killing frost tonight.

The gravel on the parking lot crunched louder than the grass had.

The minute I put foot on it, it made a noise that sounded — to me, at least — like an entire regiment charging down a gravel bed. I jumped back and stood on the grass, waiting. Waiting for what? For workmen to come and replace the gravel with bark? I took two steps out on the gravel, brave Porter, bold Porter.

A voice behind me said: 'Hold it. Hands in the air, and feet right where they are. No, don't turn around.'

Crunch on the gravel, pat, pat as hands went over me, presumably looking for a gun. 'All right. You can take your hands down.'

I did, and turned, sneezing into the face of Danny Banion. True to his green-and-tan uniform, he didn't flinch or step back, but stood his ground boldly, holding a pistol on me.

'Golly,' he said. 'You.'

'What's left of me.'

'You don't look good, and that's a fact But what are you doing up here?'

I felt like saying I didn't know. But it didn't seem like a good idea. So I tried: 'I've got to see John Five.'

'That's the screwiest thing I ever heard of,' the dendrologist said. 'He doesn't want to see you. He's got a twenty-four-hour watch out to make sure he doesn't see you.'

'You searched me. I'm not armed.'

Danny Banion shook his head. 'Whoever killed Mrs. Hilliard strangled her; he didn't need a gun.'

'Do I look like I could strangle anybody, just now?'

He laughed. 'You sure don't, Porter. But Hilliard'd fire me if I let you in to see him.'

'What do you care? You're going back in the Forest Service anyway.'

He pushed his hard-brimmed Stetson back on his forehead and holstered his gun. 'I always feel like a kid playing cowboy wearing one of these damned things,' he said. 'Listen, man, you sure you aren't out of your head, running a fever? You could have pneumonia, the way you look.'

Now was the time to prove I had sales ability, the power to dominate a vis-à-vis, as some professor had called it in college. 'Banion, I'm out of my head, but not with a temperature. The minute I show my nose in town, I'm pinched for a murder I didn't commit. John Five, Mr. Hilliard — '

'Call him anything you want to,' Danny said. 'Like you said, I'm quitting this tin-soldier job, heading for the tall timber. But I can't figure out how you know it.'

I went back to my theme. 'John Five couldn't have liked Edith any more than I did. No man could who'd been married to her awhile. He's the man with the power, the money; maybe he'll give me a hand. If he doesn't, I'm no worse off than I am now. I couldn't be.'

The Stetson dipped backward and forward as he nodded. The sky was purplish-black now. Danny Banion said: 'Maybe if he sees you, he'll call the cops, and I won't have to run a night patrol. It's going to be a stinker out. Still . . . '

'Down in town, they're saying maybe you killed Edith . . . for John Five . . . and enough of his money to make up for the size of a Forest Service paycheck.'

The big forester took a step forward, and I thought he was going to sock me. Then his laugh rolled out, hearty and frank. 'Forest Service pay's not so bad. And I got it figured out where you heard that screwy story: Janey Dandler.'

The noise I made was approximately, 'Oh.'

'Sure,' Danny Banion said. 'Crosley got a two-way report from one of our jeeps, working down the bridle path you probably got in here on. Picked up a dame with a sprained ankle, walking back from a tough date. When I heard it was Janey Dandler, I kind of wondered. The only date she ever found too tough would be maybe an honest wrestler.'

I made my noise again: 'Oh.' Or maybe, 'Ugh.'

'For a guy that Andy McLane thinks is a hot shot, you chase some funny dames.'

My vocal cords got more talented. 'She has a grudge against Otto McLane for beating up and framing her boyfriend. She wants me to get Mac for false arrest, to give him some trouble, like the kind he dishes out.'

Danny Banion tilted his hat forward again and nodded against the growing gloom. 'Sure. She has a grudge against me, too, for knocking Red clear across the street once when he was drunk and picking on me. He's strictly a no-good, Porter. And Mac didn't frame him; he just couldn't get enough evidence to bring Red to trial.'

'How about some kind of salesman over in the next county who confessed to robbing whoever it was that was robbed?'

Danny Banion looked at the sky. 'It's a hell of a night to stand out in the cold hashing up the affairs of Janey Dandler and her Red . . . That was just hacky talk, the salesman and his confession. Janey wanted Mac to run over there and pinch every salesman in sight, but it was just hacky talk; cab drivers are a bunch of old women for gossiping. No, Red rolled Freddy Hughes as sure as Freddy's next drink . . . Come on down to the estate office, and I'll call the police to come get you.'

He reached out for my elbow. I let him take it; he had the gun, and I didn't have anything but a cold and a faint hope that he'd help me. 'Banion, give me a break. Five minutes with John Five wouldn't hurt anybody, especially with you there to grab me if I got rambunctious.'

The dendrological brain chewed on that. Finally he said, 'Andy thinks you're the king of the woods, and I never knew her to be far wrong.' Faith died hard in that big man. 'Okay. If you slap him with a feather or throw a powder puff at him, it's both our necks. His money swings big weight around here.'

'Maybe you can teach me dendrology in our prison cell.'

His hand on my elbow propelled me towards the house. 'I don't know why everybody thinks being a dendrologist's so funny. It's what I am; a guy who majored in dendrology at forestry school. It's one of a half dozen branches of forestry, and it doesn't sound any sillier than silviculture, does it?'

I had to admit it didn't.

The front door of Mt. Hilliard was locked. Danny Banion fished a big ring of keys out of his windbreaker and opened it, and we went in. A wave of heat met us; it was the finest thing I have ever felt. I loosened Janey's muffler so as to enjoy it on the swollen glands of my neck. Then I sneezed twice, while Danny Banion knocked on the walnut door of a room off the big entrance hall. The door opened, and at last I got to see John Five.

He wasn't eight feet tall; he wasn't coated with platinum, or even gold. He was just a man of medium height, a little plump, a little effeminate; soft in his way of talking and moving, uncertain.

He said, 'Yes, yes, Banion, who is this?'

I remember what a salesman had told me, and looked at his lapels. Sure, the stitches were twice as close together as on any suit I'd ever worn; and that was the privilege of great wealth. I said, 'Mr. Hilliard, I'm Paul Porter.'

He said, 'Oh, my God.' He jumped back a foot. 'Get out of here. Banion, get him out! Don't let him hurt me . . . Don't hurt me, Porter. I haven't done anything to you!'

Danny Banion's voice was that of a male nurse, and since Danny wasn't the male nurse type, it was easy to see why he was quitting this soft and well-paid post. 'Mr. Hilliard, I searched him. And I'll grab him if he needs it.'

John Five was blinking at me as I would blink at a caterpillar six feet long.

'You're Porter. The — ' He broke off.

'The murderer, Mr. Hilliard? But I'm not. Mr. Hilliard — ' The respectful use of his name seemed to calm him. 'Mr. Hilliard, I'm an innocent man, being framed. The only thing I ever did wrong was marry Edith. You did as bad yourself.'

His eyes popped a little, in the soft light that came from the fanned glass over the front door. He said, 'Come, now, you can't talk about Mrs. Hilliard that way.'

This was so silly I almost breathed naturally. 'She used to be Mrs. Porter.'

The hand that came up to brush at his face was remarkably firm-looking. Perhaps that came from holding the reins on all his horses. But his gesture was ridiculous; as though cobwebs entangled his face.

'Mr. Hilliard, I have to find out who killed her. Or they'll kill me.'

He said, 'Well, do come in, Mr. — '

'Porter. Paul Porter. I told you.'

'Of course.'

He stepped back and walked into his study, not looking to see if Danny Banion and I followed him. Danny shut the door, and John Five turned to the right and went into a small room with leather furniture, leather lampshades, Navaho rugs on the floor. There were silver cups on the bookshelves but no books, and photos of horses on the walls. This was a den. I never knew anyone who had a den behind a study, but apparently John Five liked to retreat.

Danny Banion said, 'He was walking in here, not sneaking or anything. When I jumped him, he neither put up a fight nor ran away. He said he wanted to talk to you. I didn't see the harm.'

'No, no.' John Five dropped into a leather chair, very shiny-looking, very soft. There were several other chairs, and they looked very inviting, but if I sat on one he might be afraid my poverty would rub off on the leather.

I said, 'Just five minutes of your time, Mr. Hilliard. You might help me. I don't think anybody can, but you're my last chance.'

He seemed pleased. I don't suppose anyone had ever wanted to lean on him before in his whole life, except financially. 'I don't see — ' he said. He stopped as though wondering where that sentence should have gone. He tried another. 'You shouldn't hold a grudge against me. Edith was already divorced when I met her, out in Nevada. I was buying quarter horses.'

Danny Banion's patient voice said, 'He isn't armed, and he's just about pooped out — exhausted, Mr. Hilliard. Doesn't seem to be any danger.'

'No, no, Banion. Hadn't you better be seeing to the night watch?'

Danny Banion shrugged, and managed not to smile. Since the watch was being kept to see that I stayed out, and I was now in, there was a certain amount of pointlessness involved. But John Five was paying the bills.

I winked at Danny Banion as he exited in a semi-military manner. His lip quirked a little. I'd gotten to like him awfully well in our few minutes together; if Andy McLane really preferred me, it seemed she was being kind of silly.

John Five squinted at me, waved at a chair, and I sat down with a sigh.

12

John Five went around turning lights on and off until he stopped squinting. 'Sherry, Mr. Porter?'

'If I can have a cracker or something with it. I'm about beat.'

He looked at me directly and said, 'You do have a bad cold. This is no time of year to be out without your hat and coat,' as though he were my old aunt. He opened a knotty pine door, and there was a little icebox. He put a plate of cheese next to me, brought crackers and the glass of sherry; stood, indecisive a moment, opened a door, went into a tiny lavatory, brought back a box of tissues and put them next to me, too. It was the damnedest performance any suspected murderer ever saw.

He said: 'A cold's the worst thing in the world,' and sat down opposite me. Then he took out his handkerchief and held it in front of his nose and mouth. 'I certainly don't want to catch your cold.'

I ate cheese, I gulped the warming sherry, I blew my nose; the last was the greatest pleasure. 'Mr. Hilliard, I'm being killed by coincidence.'

Again, that wavery gesture of the strong left hand. 'I don't understand talk like that. I'm a very plain-spoken man myself. A businessman.'

I had heard different. But I looked at his clear eyes, his clear skin, his white teeth and made myself look pleasant. 'By sheer chance, I was in Lowndesburg when Edith was killed. By sheerer bad luck, I was up here, at Mt. Hilliard.'

He nodded. 'I don't know that I like that,' he said. 'We don't encourage tourists up here, you know. Why, last year, some people wanted to picnic in my finest grove of dogwoods.'

'I came here on business, to see you. To sell you a terracer.'

'Oh, now, really, Mr. Porter. I don't even know what a terracer is. Why in the world should I want one?'

'You own land and horses. With a Hydrol Terracer and a small tractor — say a D-30 — you could raise all the hay and grain your horses need.'

He seemed interested. 'My land's quite hilly.'

'That's what a terracer is for. It lets you use steep land without subjecting it to erosion. For instance, you could run a long, narrow contour all through your woods; raise spring barley or any other small grain on it, then turn it under and it would be a fireguard the rest of the year, protecting your woods.'

He chewed his lip. 'Not bad. Could you arrange a free demonstration?'

I hit the leather arm of my chair with my palm. 'Damn it, Hilliard, I'm not here to sell terracers. I just told you all that to prove that I had a legitimate reason to come up here yesterday.'

'Yes, yes.' He had that vague look about him again; I must remember not to frighten him with loud noises. 'Spent an awful lot of money on forage last year. Timothy hay, in particular. Just bulk, you know, not much nourishment in it, but the horses . . . ' He grinned suddenly. 'I'm not as scatterbrained as all that. I'm

210

trying to remember, someone tried to sell me a dingbat like that, once before. If he'd explained it the way you did, I'd have bought it.'

'All right, Mr. Hilliard. But I — '

'Don't you see?' He was very patient. 'I suppose you don't, what with the cold, and gulping down sherry the way you are. If someone knew that you'd be sent here to close a terracer sale, it would be a way of setting up a suspect to take the blame for Edith's murder.' He yawned. 'I certainly regretted marrying her, didn't you? I guess that's why the police were so fussy about making me establish an alibi for yesterday. Anyway, McLane and that state captain made me go with them while I interviewed the men I was with yesterday. I got myself clear. I guess you weren't so lucky.' He went on: 'Yes, setting up a date for you and me to talk terracing — and killing her at the same time, right here — one of us would be sure to hang for it.'

I had been sitting here, thinking he was a dope — and he had put the killer right in my lap. And done it in a dopey way.

A woman who looked like Edith could have any man in the world. She'd had me, she'd had rich Hilliard. She'd had another guy, and laughed him off — and he'd killed her.

'Mr. Hilliard, who was Stayne?'

'Stayne, Stayne? I don't know any Stayne. I was at a horse show last month, lost out in the green hunter class to a man named Stone — no, it was a woman, Mrs. Hilary Stone. But I don't know any — Stayne, did you say?'

'Edith's name before she married me. Edith Stayne, when she came to work where I was working.'

He nodded, but he was being vague again. 'Yes, yes, I remember that. I was introduced to her — I mean, when we were introduced — a lady is never introduced to a man, is she? — she was Mrs. Stayne Porter.'

I sneezed twice into John Five's Kleenex, then coughed once. He moved away from me nervously. 'Very distinguished,' I said, when I could say anything. 'Mrs. Stayne Porter. Very upper-class. Only, who was Stayne? The state police are pretty sure that wasn't her maiden name. She must have been married before.'

John Five chewed his upper lip and considered this. 'Poor Stayne,' was his conclusion. So now we knew who Stayne was: the third member of our club. Then the vagueness rolled back for a moment. He said, 'All you have to do, Mr. Porter, is find out who sent you up here, and you'll find he's the murderer.' He yawned. 'I presume you'll find he's this Stayne fellow, too. Yes, yes. Under another name, of course. You don't suppose Edith had been carrying on with him all the time, do you? While she was married to me, and to you, too, of course. I'd not like to think that, but women, you know. I mean, if he was poor, and — are you rich, Mr. Porter?'

I said that I managed to eat every day.

He stared at me. I don't think he'd ever heard that some people don't eat. Then he laughed. I'd made a funny. 'Do you have any horses?'

'Too bad. I find them the most diverting of occupations. I do my best thinking in the saddle. You really ought to take it up.'

I promised that I would. 'But this Stayne thing, Mr. Hilliard.'

'I can't help you there. Really, it's up to you. As I say, just think back to who told you to see me. Who sent you to this part of the country at all.'

It should have been simple to figure out. But in the condition I was in, nothing was easy; I felt like leaning back in John Five's fine chair, going to sleep and letting the police come and get me. I made a superhuman effort to keep my eyes open. 'Why, of course, everything in our company starts with the president, Harvey Planne. He told me to take a turn through the northern midwest, or I wouldn't be here.'

'Any chance he could be this chap Stayne?' John Five asked. He chuckled. 'I'm quite like those district attorneys on television, don't you think?'

Through the fog I made an answer. 'Harvey Planne's father is well known in Chicago, has been for years. Unless Harvey used a false name — no. He was still in the Air Force overseas when I met Edith, had been since she was too young to marry.'

'They're not always the age they say they are,' John Five said, his brain yawing like a sailboat again. 'Chap I know goes in for palominos; can't say I admire his taste. Got into serious trouble. Woman looked nineteen and was only fourteen; lied to him of course, cost him a pot of money.'

I took another sip of his sherry. My throat tickled and I lit a cigarette, which should have made me cough more, but didn't. 'No,' I said. 'It's not Harvey Planne. And he wasn't here, because I talked to him on the phone last night. Nobody knew I was coming to Lowndesburg. Nobody. I saw the sign at the crossroads and remembered we had that terracer here, and — like that — made up my own mind.'

John Five sighed. 'It was such a good idea.' He sounded as though he didn't have many ideas, and hated to see one wasted. 'Ah, well.'

'No,' I said. 'I just came into town and

called McLane, and then I phoned the distributor in the city and — '

John Five had made a sort of noise. I broke off and looked at him curiously. 'Otto McLane? But he's the fellow tried to sell me the terracer once before.'

'Sure, he's the only agricultural dealer in town.'

'Don't like the fellow,' John Five said with an unusual show of firmness. 'Please, be sure and turn your head when you sneeze. I hate colds! No, I don't like Otto McLane. Impudent little upstart. Gave me a ticket for parking in front of the firehouse, and I'd left my keys in the car. If they wanted it moved, they could have moved it.'

'Nobody seems to love Mac in Lowndesburg,' I said. 'He only knows one way of being a cop, and that's the big-city way. I can see it wouldn't sit so pretty in a tiny town. One of your dear citizens down in Lowndesburg even suggested that he killed Edith. Then she changed her mind and suggested that you had her killed. By Danny Banion.'

'Oh, no, I wouldn't do that. Why,

Banion could blackmail me for a fortune.'

'Not without indicting himself.' I helped myself to another cracker, another swallow of sherry.

John Five's simple face lighted up. 'You know, you're right. If he exposed me, think what he would do to himself! I never thought of that.'

'You didn't have Danny do it, did you?'

Polite laugh. 'No. I wouldn't have used Banion, anyway. My personal groom, the one who takes the horses to the shows, used to be a gunman in prohibition days. Say, shall we have him in? He tells marvelous stories.'

I sighed, starting another series of sneezes. John Five jumped up and moved hastily out of range, though I twisted my head away and covered my nose with Kleenex.

Then his brain skidded back into the road. He said, 'Porter, are you stupid or frightened?'

I said, 'Both, I suppose,' which seemed frank enough.

'I don't care much whether Edith's murderer is caught or not, except that I suppose it's bad for the whole community for a murderer to go at large. Don't you think so? But I've told you who did it, and you don't seem disposed to take any action at all.'

I half-expected him to add that he didn't know what the lower classes were coming to. 'Very sorry, maybe this cold's frozen my brain.'

'McLane,' he said. 'Otto McLane.' He looked around cautiously, but there were no police spies in the trophy shelves.

'Because he gave you a parking ticket?'

'My dear fellow. Who else knew you were coming up here, and at what time? Who told you what time to come here?'

'A woman down in town suggested Mac for about the same reasons you have — she doesn't like him. But she dismissed the idea as crazy. Murderers usually have a motive, or so I've heard.'

John Five nodded. 'Of course, he knew her. Everyone in Lowndesburg knows the Hilliards, of course. She was on a Civil Defense Committee with him, too. I made her join. Our position here, you know, demands that we participate in village activities. And then, there should be someone on every committee like that to see that not too much money is spent.'

'Otto McLane, Mr. Hilliard.'

But the boat had yawed again. 'Taxes are frightful,' John Five said. 'In a way, it's a good thing I don't have a son; there wouldn't be a thing to leave him. If I told you the tax I pay on Mt. Hilliard, you wouldn't believe it. School tax and road tax, gasoline tax, inheritance tax, income tax . . . it's communism, that's what it is.'

'Edith's murder. Otto McLane.'

He shifted sails and came back into the channel. 'Well, the minute she was killed, your state policeman found out she hadn't been born Edith Stayne, didn't he?'

I had to admit that. I was beginning to get disgusted with the whole conference; there was something gruesome about Edith's two ex-husbands quietly talking over her death. One of us should have missed her, at least. Him. He was being Mr. D.A. again. 'You admit McLane is a policeman.'

Sneezing, I nodded. When I could

speak, I said, 'A good one.'

'So he found out Edith had been married to a man named Stayne. And he got in touch with Stayne, and Stayne paid him to kill her.'

He had figured all this out because Mac had given him a parking ticket once. He wouldn't let it go.

'You admit that no one but Mac knew you were coming here just when you did,' he said.

'Mac and his daughter.'

'Ridiculous. Miss McLane a murderer? I'd never believe it.'

'I wouldn't either,' I said. I was very tired. 'I didn't mean to imply it.'

John Five started trotting around the little room. 'Too bad about her,' he said. 'Nice woman; be hard on her to find her father's a criminal. But I suppose policemen's families are more hardened than other people. Do you suppose so?'

There wasn't any sense in answering him. Two people had tried to help me besides Andy. Janey Dandler and John Five. Both of them had mentioned McLane. Probably if John Five knew about the Queen of the Hackers, he'd change his mind sooner than be associated with such low company.

So why not? I asked my rheumy brain. Why not Otto McLane? True, my first impression of him had been one of great liking. But when a man has a daughter who is a pretty woman, and a young man happens to need a pretty woman, said young man is going to stretch like a toy balloon to like the father. True, also, that there seemed the remotest connection between Mac and Edith.

But I was stopped in all other directions. Well, at least I could make some effort to find out if there was any connection. It would be doing something, and I felt intensely that I had to do something or go, framed, to the chair.

So I gave in to John Five, which was a little like losing a wrestling match with a three- week-old kitten. I said: 'Mr. Hilliard, I think you're right. If you'll lend me a car, I'll go downtown and try and hang it on Mac.'

'A car? Really, a car? I don't know.'

Patience, understanding and conviction

oozed into my voice. 'Your cars are known all over the county. In one, I'm not likely to be stopped. And if I am stopped, it might be by a policeman who doesn't know me, or you, and maybe I could bluff through.'

'I'm pretty well known. My picture is in all the horse-show magazines frequently.'

'Admittedly, I'm taking a chance. But without a car, I'm throwing the game.'

He pondered this awhile. 'Do you have a driver's license?' he asked finally. 'You see, my insurance is invalid if I lend the car to anyone without a driver's license.'

Someone defined experience as what you get when you're looking for something else. Patience is what you learn under the same circumstances. So I hauled out my license and my insurance cards, and finally satisfied him. He went with me out of the inner den and through the study to the hall, a long distance for John Five to go with a common man.

In the hall he pressed a button, and a grayish man in a blackish suit popped out from the inner reaches of the castle. 'Call Banion and tell him to meet Mr. Porter at the garages. He's to let Mr. Porter have the station wagon.'

The butler said, 'Yes, Mr. Hilliard.' Unlike his appearance, his accent was pure mideastern. John Five turned back into his double-barreled retreat without wishing me good luck or goodbye or good anything at all. The butler opened the front door, asked me if I knew where the garages were, and shut the door behind me. I heard the jingle of the bolt being shoved home.

It was fully dark now, and as cold as Alaska. I went around the house as I had done yesterday, in my carefree youth. Floodlights played on the garages, and Danny Banion, gun strapped over a forest-green short-coat, was unlocking a stall.

'My God, you look awful,' was his way of making me feel better. 'Want me to loan you an overcoat?'

'There's a heater in the car, I'm sure. You're not a bad guy, Danny.'

He swung the big door up. Inside, a station wagon gleamed. He said, 'I was all right once, and I will be again, when I get

223

to where a tree isn't a post for scratching John Five's back. I can't give you a gun, but anything else?'

'Tissues.'

'In the glove compartment,' he said. He sighed. 'The chauffeurs put fresh boxes there every time they polish the cars, which is once a day. Where to, Porter?'

'Down into Lowndesburg. I've gotten so I feel naked without my head in a lion's mouth.'

Danny Banion nodded. 'I didn't know whether you knocked off Mrs. John Five or not. But no guy that Andy liked would have killed her grandfather. So I'm for you.'

I wanted to get into the station wagon and start the heater. But here, in the garage, we were sheltered from the wind. 'Nobody killed Mr. Gray,' I said. 'I was with him. Mac played a dirty trick on him, and the old man shook himself to death.'

Danny Banion shrugged. 'Mr. Gray and Mac squabbled a lot, but I always thought they liked each other. Well, on your way. In ten minutes I got to go saddle a horse and ride around the home place. Security.' He spat on the garage floor and walked out into the night. When I pulled out, I saw him swinging the garage door shut.

13

Nobody stopped me on the way into Lowndesburg, but twice I passed road-blocks on the exits. My spirits lifted as the heater took hold; I was headed for the police station, and it seemed a safe thing to do. The roadblocks indicated that nobody was fool enough to think I'd head into Lowndesburg, or into the jail if I was still there.

Lieutenant Gamble must be going nuts, I thought; such a good cop, and unable to find a full-sized man in a child-sized town. But I was hardly in the business of preserving the amour-propre of state policemen. I was hardly in business at all.

A stop light and a street lamp came together, and I was halted under the latter. My hands on the wheel caught my eye; they were stained black. Fingerprint powder. I was sick to my stomach. I should have thought of it; this was the four-hole station wagon in which Edith was strangled.

Some minion would catch John Five-ish hell for not doing a better cleaning job. But me, I wanted to step out of the car, and run. The death, and the person who had died, came unbearably close for a moment.

A recurrence of coughing and sneezing combined with my nausea to double me over in the seat, down against the wheel. I was dimly aware of a car pulling alongside, more than dimly aware that if there was a car, I'd have to control myself.

The driver had his window down and was peering at me. I un-cranked my right-hand window.

'You all right, mister?'

I nodded, my eyes streaming. 'Sudden cold. Takes me bad.'

'Better get home and to bed.' The light changed and he pulled ahead of me. He hadn't recognized me. I probably didn't look human.

I wiped my eyes with John Five's tissue and drove on, too. I tried to think of anything but Edith.

During my months on the road, I had read a lot of detective stories. I don't go for anything much heavier; and reading passed the time more cheaply than sitting on a chrome bar stool, spending money.

So I had become a sort of expert on crime stories. The people in them suffered, they knew fear and apprehension, they were shot at sometimes; but they never had my trouble.

I was trapped by my own stupidity, my own inaction. Where a private eye — at least a fictional one, and I didn't know any others — would have thought of a dozen things to do, and done them to exhaustion and success, I couldn't think of anything, really. Where an amateur sleuth would have had a handful of suspects to track down and confront, I had only one: Otto McLane.

So I wheeled Edith's station wagon down into town and started looking for him. I didn't expect to have much trouble; he was certainly looking for me, too. He and every other cop in the world. Even a dope such as I was knows where to look for a police chief.

I drove to City Hall. It was past dark now, but City Hall Square was the only part of Lowndesburg that was lit; there, I had no trouble seeing. The hotel and shop lights added to the glow provided by the municipality's high globes. It wasn't bright as day, but it was brighter than my mood.

Sneezes and chills still racked me. I parked where I could watch the entrance to the basement police station, and left the motor running while I tried to size up the situation, using the brains I'd been given. They didn't seem adequate.

There were no state police cars in sight. Maybe there'd been an earthquake or a tornado at the other end of the state; maybe my future messmates at the state penitentiary were rioting.

I glanced at the ammeter on the car. The idling motor wasn't charging the battery; I had the fan on, the heater going full blast. If I turned the heater off, I'd freeze, and I had an idea that if I turned the fan off, I'd suffocate; so I put my foot on the gas pedal to keep the battery from running down, which meant that pretty soon I'd be out of gas.

Obviously the police had had this car. John Five's lads hadn't had a chance to refill it with gas, if they hadn't wiped off the fingerprint powder.

Something was going to have to be done soon, and there wasn't anybody but me to do it. Stupid, law-abiding me. I watched City Hall. No police cars around. Nor Mac's car. There were some sedans and coupés on the other side of the square, near the movie house, but they didn't look in any way official. There was a lit window in the police basement, and there was a glow from the firehouse around the corner . . .

It looked safe enough, but I couldn't be sure. Maybe I ought to just take John Five's car and try and get through the roadblock. Maybe in a few years someone would confess to killing Edith, and I could come out of hiding again.

Suddenly I laughed at myself. Of course. There was a radio in John Five's car. There would be. The dashboard clock said four minutes to the hour, and news broadcasts come on the hour . . .

I shot an extra minute of electricity to be sure the clock was right — though being John Five's clock, it wouldn't dare be wrong. The tubes warmed, the set hummed, a disc jockey promised to rejoin me in five minutes, and I got a break; the newscast was local, rather than national.

The announcer was a woman with a lilting flute-type voice designed to be distinctive, to make you remember her. She said that three people had been killed in traffic accidents in the state, making the year's toll nine hundred and forty-two dead as against nine hundred and thirty-six on this day last year. She said that a warehouse had burned down in Libertyville, at an estimated loss of two hundred and six thousand dollars.

She said that at the quarter, one basketball team was twenty-two points ahead of another.

She said that a man described as Paul Porter, alleged by the police to be 'the most cold-blooded killer ever to operate in this state,' had gone to earth in a motel in Mublenville, a hundred miles north of his scene of operations in Lowndesburg. State police, National Guard and special auxiliaries had surrounded the area, and a mobile public address system was being brought in to demand Porter's surrender. Sheriff —

I switched it off. The majesty of the law was, for the moment, aiming its guns at another innocent bystander. It would be nice if I could say that I worried about him, that I hoped he wouldn't get himself killed by some fumbling fool with a gun, but the truth is I was thinking about myself.

I switched the motor off, too, and climbed out of the station wagon, strolling across the last year's grass of the courthouse lawn to the blue light.

Knowles was alone in the police office; he was reading a magazine under the unshaded light over Otto McLane's desk. The magazine lay flat on the desk, and he held it in place with the stump of his right arm, turned the pages with his one set of fingers. He looked up when I came in.

'Evening, Sergeant.'

He flipped the magazine shut. It was a

book for gun fanciers. Without any apparent surprise, he said: 'Come on in. It's a quiet night; they haven't rounded up a single D and D yet.'

'D and D?'

'Drunk and disorderly. My regular customers.'

'Before you ask, I didn't kill Mr. Gray. In fact, I haven't killed anybody.'

Knowles stood up, wriggling his shoulders as though they ached. 'Nothing to me. Cops round 'em up, I hold them. With more or less success.'

'I gather I'm no longer out on bail.'

'Naw. Mac's got the estate tied up. Andy tried to bail you, but there was some kind of technicality. Anyway, the judge denied her, for all Henry Lighton's spouting off.'

I sat down on the straight chair he usually used. I sneezed. I had forgotten to bring the tissues in from the car. He opened a desk drawer and shoved a box at me.

'So?' I asked intelligently.

'So you're a fugitive, pal. But like I say, it's nothing to me. I'm not a sworn police officer, just a civilian employee of the department.' He touched his ten-cent-store badge awkwardly. 'This doesn't mean a thing.' He moved from behind the desk. 'Coffee?'

'I need your help, Sergeant Knowles.'

He shook his head. 'I wondered why all the sergeants. I'm just a janitor, Porter.'

'Then I need a janitor's help.'

For a moment the glaring light brought something into his face: strength, maybe even cruelty, a reminder of what he must have been before his accident. But it faded, or maybe had only been a trick of lighting or of my watery eyes. 'Like I said, nothing to me. I just hold them. I don't pick them up, and I don't help them, either. You want that coffee? You look frozen.'

'I hear they have me surrounded up north. Yeah, I'd like the coffee.'

He went over to his hot plate and got down two thick mugs from the shelf above it. He poured. 'That motel thing? That always happens. Some hawk-eyed citizen spots your man; some bright-badge sheriff sees a chance to get his picture in the papers.'

'Still, if it wasn't for that, this place could be covered with cops.' I shook my head for no cream or sugar.

Knowles said: 'That's what you think. Wet roads — there's cops working traffic. A fire here or there, and the nearest state trooper goes in to see the sightseers don't run over the hoses. Night like this, there'll be a couple of attempted holdups, and three fights in unincorporated territory. All state police business.'

'Still — '

'Ah, the state probably loaned a sergeant, a corporal, and four troopers to that sheriff up in Muhlenville. For various reasons. Yeah, it cuts down. Gamble and McLane are each holding down a roadblock they'd rather have a trooper handle.'

He made pretty good coffee. I drank it hot enough to burn my tongue, and said that I still needed his help.

Knowles looked at the ceiling. 'Tell your story,' he said. 'Where's the harm?'

'Two people — who I'm sure aren't working together — would like to see

Otto McLane hang for killing my wife. My ex-wife.'

He set down his cup and wiped his lips with the back of his hand. 'Screwy.'

'I thought so, too. Maybe I still think so. But I've got to be sure. And the only way I can be sure is to find out how much connection there was between Mac and Edith.'

Knowles nodded. 'Yeah,' he said. 'Mac's no guy to do anything on impulse. I mean, he's getting screwy — losing his youth hurts him worse than me losing my arm hurts me — but even if she maybe laughed at him, called him an old man, he wouldn't strangle her. He's right inside the letter of the law, that cop.'

I said wearily: 'One more country heard from. It's what everybody says about Mac. But if he knew her well, if he had time to plan — '

Knowles drained the cup. 'I got to go in the cells to wash the cups. No running water out here. Why, mister, it's not for the likes of a janitor to criticize a police chief. Chief McLane is a fine man. Very careful. Writes everything down. Files everything, right in that file by his desk. Yes, sir, you'll never catch our chief doing anything slipshod. You through with that coffee?'

I nodded, handed him my cup. He peered into it.

'Needs a good scrubbing.'

His hand was big that it held both cups and the coffee pot handle without effort. He trudged to the cells and through the unlocked iron door, then to the last lockup, clear in the back. The pot clattered, and then water was turned on.

There was the filing case; here was I. I got there fast, but for a moment my thoughts were back in the cells. How does a one-armed man hold a cup still while he scrubs it?

Then I had the file open. Headlights, Cracked, Citations for. Highway Jurisdiction.

Hilliard, Edith Stayne. I took out the folder.

Letter to Las Vegas attorneys. Letter to the Chief of Police, Moberly, Missouri. I glanced at that one. It was asking for whereabouts of and any information concerning Carl Stayne.

Letter to Carl Stayne, on 119th Street, New York City. Are you divorced? Would like to know whereabouts of your former wife. Letter from Carl Stayne . . .

Clump of Knowles's feet coming back. I slid the folder back into its place, and closed the filing case. I had enough. There was a connection between Mac and Edith. A great big, fat connection. Mac had been looking into her past. Otto McLane was a blackmailer. There was no other explanation possible; there wouldn't have been any other explanation if my brain had been rested and virus-free.

Knowles put the pot and coffee cups into a cupboard and turned to me. I guess my face was pretty transparent; he swore with fervor.

'I'm going, Sergeant.'

He said heavily, 'I couldn't stop you.'

'No. And thanks.'

'For the coffee? Nothing.' His hand came up and rubbed at his face. It hit him hard, I guess; I suppose he'd been a policeman all his adult life, and knowing that there were honest, almost perfect cops like Mac — for all his faults as a human being — had comforted him.

I remember Gamble when he saw Mac using his office to push motorists around; but police brutality was one thing, and police crookedness another completely. I wasn't a cop, but I felt bad, too.

I felt worse when I got outside. Andy!

This was the end of anything between us. She didn't like her father today, but she had liked him yesterday. In time, she'd probably like him again; after all, what he had done to Mr. Gray he had apparently done for reasons convincing to himself.

Apparently, but not really. As a murderer, as the guilty man in the case he was supposed to be working on, he couldn't take any chances on my getting away; I was his scapegoat.

So he had shocked Mr. Gray to death in order to frame me.

But it seemed doubtful that Andy would believe that. If I got Mac arrested, indicted, convicted and electrocuted, she probably wouldn't believe it. She'd think

I'd framed her father, and that was the end.

So maybe I ought to quit. Give up my life for love, as the poets say. It's a safe bet that no such poets ever had to choose between life and love. But there's no money in writing: I couldn't love you half so much had I not loved myself more.

Philosophical thoughts of a dope about to tackle a tough and experienced cop. And a cop who had me where he wanted me. I was a killer on the loose. I was, according to Flute-Voice on the radio, the worst thing that had ever hit this state, barring a cyclone or two.

Mac could shoot me on sight and get commended for it. I didn't have a gun, and had no way of getting one. I didn't have a friend. Janey Dandler had made it clear that in getting me into Mt. Hilliard she'd run out of favors. John Five had run out almost before he started. Danny Banion, Lieutenant Gamble, the bartender, Lou — who else did I know in Lowndesburg?

Mr. Gray, who'd really helped me, was dead. Mac was my enemy, on the hunt for me. Andy was her father's daughter, Henry Lighton, money's lover.

Whither, Porter? There was no answer.

Jail suddenly looked good, but not Mac's jail. Knowles was on my side, but it would be too easy for Mac to send him on an errand and fire him if he didn't go. And then I'd be dead in a cell, instead of on the first pavement Mac saw me treading.

If I could make it to Lieutenant Gamble, I'd at least live to go to prison or the chair; at least I'd survive long enough to have a trial, maybe an appeal, maybe a commutation from the governor — or was that just melodrama?

Until you have thought of a life sentence as attractive, you have not fully lived. My advice is: don't live. It hurts too much.

So I got ready to give myself up; it became my version of going on fighting.

First, I had to get away from City Hall, from the square. Sooner or later Mac was sure to come back to his office, and Mac was what I didn't want to meet.

I climbed back into John Five's car,

and started it up again. The gas gauge needle barely moved as the juice was switched on. And gas was how I measured time now; on foot I was a walking quail; which is the same as a sitting duck.

14

Away from the square, Lowndesburg was poorly lighted. I drove along, the tires humming on the damp pavement. I turned corners, I went straight awhile; the aimless wanderings of an indecisive fugitive.

Then I saw a light ahead: a market, closed, but with night lights left on, no doubt to alert Otto McLane's night man if burglars were working inside. Outside there was a phone booth.

I would phone. I would order my forces. I would go down fighting.

At which point the station wagon, which seemed as fond of me as the rest of Lowndesburg, spluttered and died. I had used up the last of John Five's gas.

Like everybody when that happens, I stepped on the clutch as quickly as possible, and I undoubtedly twisted and jerked at the wheel, trying to get more roll with body English. And like everybody, I found that what had looked like a level street was really slightly uphill. The car stopped and started to go backward, and I set the hand brake.

About two blocks to the market and the phone booth. Nothing to do but walk.

Only two minutes, maybe three, but I felt as conspicuous as an overcoat on a bathing beauty. A man as lightly clad as I was, out on a night like this, would attract a second and a third glance from any passing motorist, and my face had been in all the local papers; the mad-dog-killer.

I walked as fast as I could. I hunched my shoulders, vainly trying to look smaller, and it didn't work; the second car that passed me stopped, and the driver yelled: 'Out of gas?'

I nodded and walked on.

'Want a ride to a filling station?'

I shook my head.

The driver said: 'Hey, you're Porter.'

Janey Dandler's brother, the hacky. He pulled over to the curb and got out. He was not a very big man, but he was taller than Janey, and broader than me; what he gave away in vertical inches he made up in chest girth. He stood square in front of me. 'Thought you was up at John Five's.'

'I was. I'm not anymore.'

'Yeah. Wise guy.' He shifted his squatty bulk as I tried to step around him. 'Listen, wise guy. Stay away from Janey.'

'I don't plan on ever seeing your little sister again.'

'She's older than I am; she ain't my little sister. But I don't want you seeing her, all the same. You get me?'

'I get you. Now you get out of my way.'

Dandler shifted again. I'm not an aficionado of the prize ring, but to me he moved as though he'd worn gloves and fancy trunks in his time.

He said, 'Janey, she's got a nose for picking no-good bums. Red, and Freddy Hughes for a while, and now you. Leave her alone.'

For no reason at all, I said: 'You drove her up to see me today.'

'Sure. She's my sister. When she asks for my help, I come through. But she ain't here now, so I'm saying leave her alone.'

'Get out of my way, Dandler.'

This was spreading joy and good cheer.

He grinned a happy, jubilant grin, and rocked back on his heels a little, giving the effect that he had sunk into the pavement a quarter inch. 'Try and make me.'

The habit of being a sucker was now so ingrained in me that I threw a punch. He brought up one palm, caught my fist, and squeezed it a little before he threw it away. A little — no more than the closing of a bank vault door on it would have done.

When he threw my fist away, I went with it.

Since the sidewalk was paved, I fell on the pavement. He pulled his heels out of the concrete, walked over to stand over me, and asked me if I wanted any more.

'No,' I said. 'Less. I want a good deal less.'

But I got up. With my cold it wasn't good for me to lie on the pavement. I said: 'I was just going to phone. Do you mind?'

'Janey?'

'Good Lord, no. Can't you get an idea

through head of yours? Janey's nothing to me.'

Now, I supposed, he'd really give me the works for spurning his sister. 'She ain't?'

'No. She wanted me to mess Mac up because it would make the case against her Red look better. That's all.'

Dandler chewed on this. He finally said, 'Nothing would make that Red look better. A bum and a no-good from way back. When she was going with Freddy Hughes, the lush, Pop and me thought she couldn't sink no lower, but she did.'

'That's all there was between Janey and me. When she found out I couldn't do any better against Mac than anybody else could, she threw me away, like you did.'

Dandler chewed some more. Then he said a good word for Mac, the first I'd heard in Lowndesburg. 'Mac's not so bad. If you gotta have cops, he's not worse than the next one. I'm sorry I knocked you down.'

'That's a very flattering way of putting it. Thanks.'

'Get in the cab, and I'll drive you

around to Lou's and buy you a drink. Lou ain't so bad, neither, for all he's Red's brother.'

'I'm a fugitive from justice,' I said.

'Huh?' Then he got it. 'Oh, yeah. A lamister. Well, lie down on the floor of the heap, and I'll bring you a snort. You can use it.'

I wasn't at all sure that I could. It might thaw me, and it might melt me down to a weak puddle of indecision. But I finally nodded, on the principle that any change could be a change for the better, and got into the back seat of his cab.

He made the springs creak a little as he got behind the wheel; he was certainly solidly built.

We drove a little while, then stopped where lights streamed down on me, curled on the floor. Dandler got out, went away, came back after a while, and started the motor.

He tossed something over his shoulder and I picked it up. It was a half-pint of cheap rye. I sucked on it and felt warmer, or at least less cold. The car stopped again.

We were in front of the closed market. 'You was going to phone,' he said. 'Want me to get gas for that station wagon?'

'Sure. But why?'

'I knocked you down,' he said, persisting in his flattering distortion of the facts. 'I swung when I shoulda been listening. Pop says I'm too fast with my fists. I'll get a can of gas from our garage.'

'Thanks. There's probably a reward for me by now.'

His short figure was as erect as de Gaulle's. 'Nobody in our family ever yelled copper, and nobody never will. Not even on a punk like Red.'

If I had known Latin, I would have translated his statement and had it carved on a Dandler family shield. It was as noble a sentiment as has ever been voiced.

So now I could make my phone calls. There had been a time in my life when using a phone was a simple matter, but since my arrival in Lowndesburg, nothing was simple. Not even blowing my nose. I had again forgotten to bring tissues from the stalled car.

My first time got me Henry Lighton. By luck, he was at his office; the phone book listed it, his farm, and an apartment in town. I told him who I was, and then proved it by a series of magnificent sneezes and coughs.

His response was gratifying. 'Where are you? I've worried myself baldheaded about you. Don't you know you're in a position to be shot on sight? The streets are full of sharp-eyed young troopers with virgin guns.'

'I'm in a booth. Do you think the police have your phone tapped?'

His voice was a snort coming at me from the night. 'They'd better not. Where are you? Can I come and pick you up?'

'I want to talk to you. I want to talk to Andy. After we talk, I want to give myself up to Lieutenant Gamble.'

His polished voice was dubious. 'I don't know about Andy. Her grandfather — '

'Try her,' I said, and started to hang up.

'All right. Don't come here; too close to City Hall. My apartment.'

I checked his street address against the map in the back of the book. It looked easy to get to.

I wanted to get out of the booth, but I had to shoot another dime. I called the state police number on the cover of the phone book. Gamble was out. I got a man at his desk, a Corporal Something-or-other. 'This is Paul Porter. I want to talk to Lieutenant Gamble right away.'

'Now hold on, Mr. Porter. It may take me some time to get the lieutenant.'

'I'm not holding on. Phones can be traced.'

'Call him at 3-7717.' That was one alert corporal.

My third dime got me Lieutenant Gamble. It sounded like a railroad station, but he answered the phone himself. I could hear lots of other voices in the background, all men.

'I think I can trust you, Lieutenant,' I said. 'If I tell you where I'll be in twenty minutes, will you keep it to yourself and give me the twenty minutes?'

'Now, Mr. Porter — '

'Yes, or no?'

'Yes.'

'Henry Lighton's home in town, not the farm. Bring some of your men if you want to, but nobody else.'

'Oh?'

'I won't discuss it. I'm hanging up, and you can go back to looking for me.'

'You're not easy to find, and that's a fact. Reporters from the wire services are on their way in to rib us. All right, it's a deal. Henry Lighton's in twenty minutes.'

That call had been hard to make; I was not exactly a police-loving type of citizen any longer.

The next call was almost impossible. My fingers froze and wouldn't hold the receiver; the coin wanted to go anyplace but in the slot. But it was only Knowles's calm, slightly bitter voice that answered: 'City police.'

'Is Chief McLane there?'

'Out on a call. Any message?'

'Porter, Knowles. I'm going to be at Henry Lighton's in twenty minutes. I'd rather he didn't get there before then.'

Knowles's drawl was still calm. 'Then you shouldn'ta called till you were there.

If he calls in, I gotta tell him right away.'

It was too late now. I hadn't managed this any better than I'd managed anything else in Lowndesburg.

I hung on the phone, trying to think of some way of swinging Knowles back to my side. I had called up, of course, to try and get Knowles to delay Mac for my needed twenty minutes. But Knowles had gone back to being a cop; or maybe he was resting on dead center again, a janitor as he called himself, helping no one, hindering no one.

Feebly, I said, 'It's very important to me.'

'I just take messages for the chief.'

'I know, I know, you're just a janitor.'

Down the block, the chunky figure bending over my car could only be Dandler. I started walking. The wind had shifted; the air was almost balmy. Spring was coming back to Lowndesburg; I could enjoy it from my cell.

He flipped the cover over my gas tank cap and said, 'All set. I'll give you a push to get the gas circulating.'

'And then goodbye?'

'You was right,' he said. 'Janey'd never have nothing to do with a punk like you. Put your car in second gear.'

But because he had thrown me down, or maybe because I was anti-cop, he pushed his hack against the rear bumper of the station wagon and shoved me down the street.

Before we got to the market, I remembered to turn the ignition on, and the station wagon shot ahead. In the rearview mirror I saw the cab U-turn and get away from there without waiting for any thanks. One wise Dandler.

Using the box of tissues provided by John Five, I hacked and coughed and blew my way to Henry Lighton's street, as indicated on the phone-book map. Of course, not a house number was visible, but his house was 942, and this was the nine-hundred block; it oughtn't to be hard to find.

Strictly speaking, Henry didn't have an apartment, he had a tiny house. He was just parking his car in the driveway as I came down the block. I wondered how he'd shaken off reporters and cops.

Maybe he'd told them he was out of the case. Maybe he was. But he'd been cordial on the phone.

I parked behind a little coupé and crammed my pockets with tissues. Then I got out. When I walked alongside the coupé, it was lettered 'J. F. Gray's Feed and Seed Co.' I went back to the station wagon.

Under the seat there was a crescent wrench, small enough to go in my pocket, heavy enough to knock a man out if it connected with his chin. Maybe.

Passing the coupé, I was scared all over again. But there was noplace to go but ahead. I rang the doorbell.

15

Henry Lighton had had time to get his hat and coat off. He opened the door at once. 'Man, something for sore eyes.'

'I'm sore all over, not just my eyes.'

He laughed as though I'd really been witty, and bowed me into the living room. 'Welcome to my pied-à-terre. Two rooms and bath. Paul, if you ever think of buying a farm, come to me. I've slept out there three nights in the last four months.'

'McLane's car is out in front.'

'Wrong again. That's Andy's coupé. She's here.' He laughed his pleasant laugh again. 'Can't you smell her perfume? I was kidding her about it.'

'Not with this cold.'

Andy's voice said: 'Here's a hot rum and butter for you.' She came through a door, a little kitchenette behind her. She had a copper mug in her hand, steam rising from it. Her face looked grim and drawn, as though she'd been crying.

I said, 'Thanks.'

She shook her head. 'Don't bother with thanks. You're cold and you're sick.'

I held the mug, the heat rising to tantalize me. Then I set it down. I had Dandler's liquor in me; I didn't dare take any more. 'You don't think I killed your grandfather, do you?'

She bit her upper lip. 'I don't know what to think anymore. About anything.'

'You know what Mac did. What your father did. Tried to have Mr. Gray declared incompetent. The old gentleman got so mad he had some kind of an attack. Just fell over on that pile of money.'

I reached out for her. She stepped back.

'The police say you — that you were trying to get the money. That you maybe tortured him to find out where it was. And then knocked him down when you found out it was old-fashioned bills, no good to you.'

She'd retreated as far as the wall of the little entrance hall, so I could get my hands on her shoulders.

'What police told you that? Your father?'

'What difference does it make? Dad wouldn't lie about police business.'

I closed in a little and almost had my arms around her, but she slipped past me into the tiny living room. I followed her. She had begun to cry, and I had to comfort her. Henry Lighton's dry voice stopped me. 'As I understand it, the police will be here pretty soon. Lieutenant Gamble called me. He's giving you — ' Henry Lighton glanced at a flat gold wristwatch ' — twelve minutes from now. You'd better let your love life go and talk to your attorney.' He was leaning on a little bar at the back of the room. Behind him there was a tiny combination icebox and stove, a liquor cabinet, and some highly polished glasses.

I said: 'Mr. Lighton, I didn't kill anybody — neither Edith nor Mr. Gray. I haven't any money — my car, some clothes, a couple of hundred dollars I could borrow on my life insurance, a half month's pay coming to me. But I've always made good money, and I should again. Take my case, and I'll pay you back, some way, sometime.'

He nodded his neat and shining head. 'I cost like hell. Ten thousand dollars for a murder case. Are you willing to sign a promissory note at six percent?'

'Yes, but — '

He said 'Ah, hah' with triumph. 'You don't plan to dicker, do you?'

'I was just going to say, but don't you want some proof I'm innocent?'

'Once you've retained me, you're innocent.'

Andy said suddenly, 'Your hot rum,' and went out into the hall. She came back — there were no distances in that tiny house — and said, 'Oh, Henry, it's left a ring on your lovely little table.'

Henry Lighton waved this aside. 'Don't you want your drink, Paul?'

'I had one before.'

'You'll go a long time till the next one. I won't put up bail for anybody; and it might take some time to sell your car and pay a bail bondsman. Is the car paid for?'

'Yes, but I'm trying to tell you I know who killed Edith.'

He waved his hand; the wristwatch caught the light and shot it around the room. 'Don't tell me anything till you've retained me, my friend.' He reached under the bar, brought out a folder, opened it, and laid a piece of paper out. 'I just happen to have brought a note from the office. Sign right here.'

I stood staring at him.

'Come on,' he said. 'Time's wasting. What is it Clifford Odets always has his characters say . . . ? 'I can hear the whistle blowing.''

Fascinated, I moved towards the bar. He held out a fountain pen. I took it from him. His eyes were bright, his lips a little wet. There wasn't a hair out of place on his head, not a speck of lint on his flannel suit, but he didn't look urbane anymore.

'Sign it, Paul,' he said. 'I'm your only hope.'

Andy cried, 'No,' and broke the spell.

I turned towards her. She was crying now, openly. 'Paul, there's something wrong. He looks like — like Mephisto in Faust.'

Henry Lighton's laugh was light and

clear, and thoroughly amused. 'Now we're setting our little melodrama to music,' he said. 'I always look like that when I think about ten thousand dollars. Like you, Andy, I believe in the young man; I think he's going to make big money.' He drooped a little and added sadly, 'Maybe I should've made it twenty thousand.'

A lot of talk, but of all the things he said, the one that moved me most was his saying that Andy believed in me. She must have said something to him while I was prowling around outside.

Then I remembered that I was about to alienate her forever and a month.

But I signed the paper.

Henry Lighton picked it up, waved it in the air, and kissed it. 'God, how I love money. All right, start talking. The good lieutenant will be here in a minute or so; perhaps you ought to talk fast, but clearly. If we need more time, he'll certainly give it to us; a fugitive surrendering through his lawyer is always in a strong position.'

Andy said, 'Paul, you said you know who killed Edith Hilliard.'

Henry Lighton said, 'The state's got a damned weak case on that one, anyway. Happenstance and coincidence never hung a man with a good lawyer. Or is it hanged? But the matter of Mr. Gray, that's serious. You were there, he'd just told you that you had to go back to jail, he took out of his secret cache money — under duress or not; who can prove? — which hadn't seen the light of day in thirty — odd years — a very serious set of facts.'

'But no one killed Mr. Gray. He dropped dead.'

Henry Lighton leaned his elbows on the bar and rested his chin on his hands. 'Would a jury accept that? Possibly, in view of his age. But you were alone with him. And I don't see how I can prevent that fact, and the other facts submitted above, from getting to a jury. The other case, that of Edith Stayne Hilliard, consists of allegations not facts, and these I can quite probably get barred from the record. Meaning, no jury will have to consider them.'

He straightened up and came from

behind the little bar. His walk was a saunter. I'm sure his mind had created a judge behind the little bar, a jury in Andrea, a press table in me.

'I'm a lawyer's lawyer, and no ham,' he said. 'The law, as decided by a judge, is clean and beautiful; the facts, as decided by a jury, exist in a shadowy territory, a Cloud Cuckoo Land, if you please, where anything can happen, and the most brilliant man cannot say it nay. Case against Paul Porter, in the matter of Edith Stayne Hilliard, thrown out for lack of evidence. Yes. You understand, we'll not be so lucky as to have only the local worthy who's district attorney of this county to contend with; there'll be the attorney general of the state, perchance, and quite possibly a special prosecutor, all planning to nourish their measly careers on this fat table of publicity spread before them.

'Ergo. In the matter of Edith Stayne Hilliard, no case. Then, what happens to the matter of the death of J. F. Gray? Why was the defendant there, what possible motive could he have for acting against a

lovable old man? 'Well, this, that bail — '
'But I object, your honor. The prosecution is seeking to inject matter from a dismissed case.' Double jeopardy? Perhaps, but certainly matter that could not be proved in one case cannot be testimony in another. Aha!'

Andy said, 'Henry, listen to Paul.'

But he was off again. 'Certainly there will have to be two trials. At an interval, too. By the time of the second trial, the attention of the whole country will be fastened on Paul Porter, a poor wretch in the toils of ambitious politicians. It's going to be a lovely mess.'

Andy said again: 'Paul knows who killed that poor woman, Henry.'

Henry Lighton dismissed the whole matter with one graceful hand. 'It doesn't apply any longer. I'm not going to fight facts with facts; I'm going to fight allegations with law, good solid law. No, I don't care.'

I had my eyes on Andy's lovely face. It could be mine, to kiss at will, to gaze upon in my home for the rest of my life. Men have stolen, killed, for much less beautiful objects — diamonds, oil paintings; all I had to do was keep my weak mouth shut.

And then, I couldn't. My lips opened and the words came. 'I care. She was my wife, she was a human being. Maybe she made my life miserable, wiped out my life savings — you'd call that corny, Henry — but I'm not John Five to say: 'She annoyed me, off with her head.' I care. And I don't care for her murderer to go marching around the world free.'

Henry Lighton went behind his little bar again, selected a glass and a bottle and poured himself a short straight drink. 'You should've been a lawyer, Paul. You'd have done beautifully in the magistrates' courts, or collecting small debts.'

I looked at Andy, at her glowing eyes, and I said, 'Otto McLane killed Edith.'

The glow went, and shock spread from her jawline slowly up her cheekbones to her forehead. 'Oh, Paul.'

'Hear me out. Then maybe you'll never listen to me again, because I know you, Andy; not long, but well. You're loyal. You're mad at your father now, but once he's in trouble, you'll forget that; you'll stick by him.'

Henry Lighton drank his little drink and clacked the empty glass on the bar. 'A lawyer with a fool for a client is in a better position than vice versa. Paul, you're out of your mind. Mac? Never.'

'Hear me out, counselor. One, Mac's been slipping; that was why he had to resign from the city force; that was why he resented old man Gray — I'm sorry, Mr. Gray. He's been using his badge and uniform to be unnecessarily harsh and brutal; Lieutenant Gamble and I saw him yesterday, or was it today, pushing motorists around and enjoying it.'

I stopped and looked at the two pairs of eyes that watched me. Neither of them was friendly.

But I'd bitten it off; I had to chew it. 'Two. He wanted to get out of here, out of the business that had been given to him, but not completely out of a house that wasn't his. He needed money for that.'

Henry Lighton said, 'I happen to know that Mac's pension was more than sufficient for a widower.'

'Peanuts,' I said. 'Popcorn money. He wanted the big money, the kind that makes people look up to you. Where to get it? The Hilliards, John Five and his wife, have the only big money around here. Edith looked easier than John Five. She was. He found something on her, he attempted to blackmail her, and Edith — Edith never gave a damn for anything but money, but that she loved with a love that passeth understanding.'

Andy said, 'A bush-league edition of you, Henry. I'm not going to listen to this.' Anger only accentuated her beauty.

But I went on. Henry had offered me a way out, a lawyer's door to walk through; I could have stood mute, as he would have said, and had my freedom and Andy, too; but I talked. 'Three. No one but Andy and Mac knew I'd be at Mt. Hilliard at just the hour I was.'

'Then I murdered her, and framed you?' She was trying not to cry.

'No, Mac did.'

Henry Lighton was smiling at me. 'Someone ought to collect the weird things a desperate man comes up with.

Forget it, Paul. Have no fear, Henry Lighton is here. I'll get you off with ease, without this fantastic hodgepodge.'

And Andy said, 'I don't think I can ever forgive you for even thinking of it. But just tell me one thing, Paul: how in the world could you ever connect Dad with Edith Hilliard, except as the most casual of acquaintances?'

I said: 'Go down to the little hole that Lowndesburg calls its police headquarters. Look in his file. He's got a thick folder on the background and life of Edith Stayne Porter Hilliard. He's been writing to cops all over the country getting the dope.'

My cough came back on me. I doubled over with it. Henry Lighton reached down under the bar, got a glass of water and put it on the bar; he didn't hand it to me. I got up and took it, and drank it down, blew my nose, and went on.

'He was ready. He tried to blackmail her. You didn't know Edith as I did. She never put out money; it was strictly one-way with her. She was going to expose him.'

Henry Lighton raised a hand. 'I'd be ashamed to lay trash like this before a jury,' he said. 'Conjecture, pure conjecture, and not even very logically devised. How could she expose him without exposing herself, losing her mink-lined nest at John Five's?'

'You didn't know her. All she would see was that Mac was forcing her to pay out money. She'd never have done that. You just didn't know her well enough.'

'But Henry knew her very well,' Andy said. 'Better than anybody in Lowndesburg, except John Five of course.'

'I'm one of the leading experts on the late Edith,' I said. 'On the other hand, I certainly don't know Mac as well as you do, Andy. But I should say that all he'd see was his honor about to be smirched, his reputation as a police officer destroyed. I don't know whether he loves that honor more or less than he loves you, or his own life — but I'd guess the three ranked about even with him.'

So I'd said it. I was left breathing hard; my lungs or bronchials or both were filling with the cold. 'Henry, I'll take that drink now. I've made my speech.'

He nodded absentmindedly. 'Quite a speech, too. Straight whiskey, do you?' He turned to his neat bottles, his sparkling glasses. 'I almost believe you.' He raised a hand. 'Almost, but not quite, Andrea.'

Then he was pouring me a shot. I stood up again to get it. Something had crossed my rheumy mind. I should have taken that folder out of Mac's files. By now he had probably destroyed it, my luck being what it was.

'I still say I'm not taking any of this into a public court. Your defense, Paul, will be strictly on legal grounds.'

The liquor started me off coughing again. My eyes watered, and I mopped them. 'But Mac — '

'Mac can take care of himself. Damn good care of himself,' Otto McLane said.

16

He stood in the door from the hall, a gun
held big in his hand. He still wore his
police uniform with the brass eagles on it.
I now noticed that the LPD on his lapels
did not quite cover the marks of the city's
insignia; this was his old uniform, thriftily
converted.

He said: 'Damn, Porter, you had me
fooled. I took you for a creampuff.'

The bore of the gun was big enough to
cover the whole area of Henry Lighton's
little living room. I wondered idly if it was
a .38 or .45 or maybe even bigger; the
only hand-held elephant gun in the
world.

Otto McLane was, for the moment, a
pit bull, the white kind with the
squinting, flat, pink eyes. He said: 'An old
copper like me, taken in by a set of
narrow lapels and an Italian necktie. You
got a good brain, boy. I could've made a
policeman out of you.'

Andy cried, 'Oh, God, Dad,' and buried her face in her hands, sobbing.

'Where's your fancy state trooper, Porter?' Mac said. 'I bet you phoned him to pick you up here.'

My voice was distinctly hollow. 'I don't know.'

Henry Lighton said quickly, 'Mac, if you overheard all this — and it seems you did — remember I never took any stock in it.'

I was very pleased to hear that Henry's voice was hollow, too. He seemed as frightened as I was.

Mac said: 'Have no fear, in your own words, Henry. Otto McLane's here, and he's a good cop; he takes 'em alive when he can, and he usually can.'

Andy said, 'Dad, Dad . . . '

McLane's chuckle was a growl. 'Andy, your Paul Porter made a lot of sense. How come you didn't believe him?'

Andy said simply: 'You're a lousy hay-and-grain dealer, but you're a good cop.'

'Carve it on my tombstone. And keep the hands on the bar, Henry.'

I sputtered something that was meant to be 'What?' or maybe just 'Whoosh.'

'Henry didn't believe you either, Porter,' Mac said. 'Why should he? He croaked your ex-wife.'

Henry Lighton said, 'This is double-feature night at the Fantasy Theater.'

McLane said: 'Lieutenant Gamble should get here sooner or later; there must be one guy on the state force who had a street map of Lowndesburg. I'm waiting till he goes to make my pinch. There's fewer accidents when there are two cops to cover each other. I was searching your flat here, Henry, when you and Andy came barging in. I took cover in your clothes closet — damned if you don't use perfume. I always thought it was just good soap.'

Henry Lighton said, 'I wish I had a recording of this. It seems highly saleable to the smaller television stations.'

'Sure, so long as I can see both hands on the bar.'

'Do you mind if I pour myself a drink?'

'To throw in my eye? No, thanks. I've known all along, Henry, you were in on this. Where I made my mistake ... I thought you sent for Porter to do the actual knockoff. He had a good motive for it, and I wrote you down as a guy who'd play it cool, have an alibi for the killing time.'

'Gaudy talk, Mac,' Henry Lighton said. 'And in front of two witnesses, it constitutes slander.'

I presume that my jaw was on my Italian necktie by now. Actually, I don't remember where it was.

'Sue me,' Mac said. 'Edith Hilliard liked money, but she didn't mind spending a little, Porter, to protect a lot more. So you didn't know her as well as you thought you did. An old cop usually finds out that most husbands don't know their own wives, but that ain't what we're talking about. You're a good lawyer, Henry, and you're John Five's lawyer. When he got married, you started making sure his new wife didn't have attachments that could mess up the Hilliard estate.'

'Of course,' Henry Lighton said. 'But, Mac, you're making too much of what was my plain duty.'

Mac laughed again, his pit-bull laugh. 'When you found out she was never divorced from Stayne — because she didn't want to spend money getting rid of someone who'd run out on her — it became your duty to try and shake her down, didn't it?'

Henry Lighton took the advice he would have given a client; he said nothing.

Mac kept on talking: 'She came to me. There's no private detective in Lowndesburg, and if there was, those guys are punks. She offered me a reasonable fee to get you off her neck. Incidentally, I found Stayne; did you? He's running a tire recap shop in San Diego, California. He went and divorced her in Nevada two weeks ago, at her expense — not that that makes her marriage to either Porter or John Five any better.'

Andy said, 'Dad, I never dreamed — '

'Ah, it's legal, baby; a part-time police officer can do private chores, beyond the call of his duty, and get paid for it.'

'I wasn't thinking of that,' said Andy.

Mac said, 'I told her not to tell you,

Henry, who was doing her work. That seemed to protect her; you wouldn't bump her off while you knew someone else was aware of the blackmail attempt.'

My nose started to run again. I fumbled in my pocket for tissues, and my fingers closed around the wrench. I'd put it there ages ago to protect me from Mac, when I thought Andy's car was his, in front of Henry Lighton's.

Mac said: 'When she got it in the neck — ' I could see out of the side of my eye Andy wince. ' — I just didn't know. It didn't seem like you to do anything like that. Then John Five mentions a husband named Paul Porter, and I had a Paul Porter right in town. I'd even seen him get sick when he caught a glimpse of Mrs. John Five. Whammo, I got it. She'd left him broke, she'd left him mad; you got hold of him, Henry, and offered him a little dough and your protection as a great lawyer to do something he wanted to do anyway; and he done it.'

I said, 'No, Mac, I had nothing — '

'Aw, punk, I know that. I been in there listening. It woulda worked, too, but you wouldn't powder-puff out; you kept on slugging, climbing around in the rain, and goddamn — you come up with it's me that done it.'

He'd had some culture before, but he was dropping back to the linguistic level of the beat-slogging patrolman. He said: 'You told it so good, you almost had me believing it,' and laughed his growl again. 'If you'd been in with Henry, you never woulda bothered. Of course, I had alibis all over the place; I was at a town council meeting from after you left my office till the mayor dropped me at Mr. Gray's house.'

'Oh.' That was me, the brilliant conversationalist. 'I never thought of that.'

'You done good,' Mac said. 'For an amateur. And there's your lieutenant, just pulling up in front of here. Later than a cow in a horse race.'

Henry Lighton said, 'Now that there'll be a competent officer here, I have every intention of moving my hands, Mac. You can't shoot me and claim some non-sense — '

Mac said: 'Hold it, Henry.'

Henry Lighton said, 'Hands in the air, as they say?' and started to raise them.

His suit cuffs slid back, disclosing lovely white cuffs with massive gold links. It's peculiar what you see at a time like this.

Then a tiny, tiny pistol appeared in one hand, and the manicured fingers worked for it — and I threw the wrench.

It missed Henry Lighton completely and broke a bottle of rare old Scotch on the back bar.

But Mac didn't miss; the little guy became a Doberman for jumping. The sights of the pistol came down on Henry Lighton's head, and the legal coiffure was no longer immaculate.

And Lieutenant Gamble came in with a trooper behind him, like the Seventh Cavalry in an old-time movie — only this time, the soldiers arrived just as Geronimo scalped the last settler.

Lieutenant Gamble said, 'I'm sorry, we had a flat tire, and the jack kept slipping.'

Mac straightened up from behind the bar. This time his laugh was real. He said,

'Didn't you never think of radioing for another car to pick you up, Lieutenant? They got radios in all the cop cars now, and from what I hear, they work real dandy.'

Lieutenant Gamble blushed.

Mac hauled Henry Lighton to his feet. The lawyer's eyes were opening again, but a thin trickle of blood was running towards the left one.

Lieutenant Gamble gave that a big old reaction: the Seventh Cavalry sort of inviting the Apaches to the USO for an ice-cream soda. He jumped forward and pushed Mac away from Henry Lighton and towards his trooper. 'Hold Chief McLane there.'

The trooper dropped a hand on Mac's shoulder; he was a good eight inches taller than Mac. He said, 'You won't give me any trouble, will you, Chief?'

Mac winked at me, and suddenly I felt wonderful — runny nose, scratchy throat and all. Otto McLane liked me. It was as big a laurel wreath as being asked to be secretary of state by a president you'd vote for.

Lieutenant Gamble was sort of brushing Henry Lighton off, and using his own handkerchief to mop at Henry's ruined hairdo. He said, 'There's a first-aid kit in my car, Mr. Lighton. I'll get it and patch you up, but maybe you ought to telephone a doctor to come over here. His testimony will be valuable to us later.'

Mac said: 'While you're cleaning up, Lieutenant, there's a little bitty old gun behind the bar that I'd pick up, if I was you. Your patient there was gonna plug me with it, but hell, I've rubbed up against so many rough characters in my life, the skin on my belly's probably too calloused to get hurt from a derringer.'

Lieutenant Gamble gave up his ministrations to turn on Mac, who was still calmly wearing the trooper's hand on his shoulder. 'In case you think I'm outside my jurisdiction, Chief, being inside yours, I'll remind you that there's a state statute covering incompetence, dishonesty or brutality of local officers, both county and municipal.'

'Sure,' Mac said. 'Statute 2911, and Paragraph Four covers brutality. That what you think I've been doing?'

Andy began to laugh. It started as sort of a mild giggle, and then rose and got a honking quality I didn't like; it was too close to hysteria. I went over and put my arm around her, and she leaned against me and seemed to take some comfort. She calmed down.

Despite the fact that I was still, in his eyes, the prime suspect in a murder case — and Andy could be my moll, about to slip me a rod — Lieutenant Gamble hardly glanced at us. He was busy with Mac. 'What do you call it, if not brutality, when legal counsel feels it necessary to carry a gun before conferring with a police officer sworn to keep law and order?'

'Wow,' Mac said. 'If I could fling that kind of language around, they might let me work the telephone switchboard at headquarters.' He turned his head and looked up at the trooper. 'Don't bear down so heavy, son. I'm old and frail.'

From inside my arm, Andy said, 'Stop it, Dad. You're making an enemy out of

Lieutenant Gamble, and it isn't necessary.'

'It don't matter to me,' Mac said. 'I'm
leaving the state. I got an offer to run the
plant police for a factory with more
people working in it than live in this
whole county.'

By now, something seemed to be
getting through to Lieutenant Gamble.
Mac wasn't talking like a man about to be
broken for police brutality, and Andy
wasn't talking like a woman being hugged
by a murderer, and Henry Lighton wasn't
talking period, which was perhaps the
most unusual thing of all.

The trooper took his hand off Mac's
shoulder, which called my attention to
him. From his carefully immobile face,
and the brightness of his eyes, he looked
exactly like a private about to see a
lieutenant made a damned fool, which
was exactly what he was.

Mac said: 'Henry Lighton killed Edith
Stayne Porter Hilliard Five. I got him
dead to rights. When I flung it at him, he
tried to plug me with the derringer that's
lying behind the bar, which I wish you'd

pick up. So I slugged him on the head.'

Lieutenant Gamble looked at Henry Lighton.

Henry said, 'I'm not saying anything at all. I stand mute.' But his face gave him away.

Lieutenant Gamble took a pencil out of his inside pocket and went behind the bar. He bent over and straightened up with the pencil inside the belly-gun's barrel. He laid the little gun on the bar, took an envelope out of his side pocket, and teased the gun inside the envelope with the pencil.

'I like to see a real cop work,' Mac said. 'Beautiful.'

Lieutenant Gamble looked at his trooper. 'You don't take shorthand, do you? Well, go out to the car and radio for a trooper who does. I'll want to take Chief McLane's statement down.'

'Later,' Mac said. 'Later. I'll meet one of your boys down at my office and give him the whole thing. It's a watertight case.'

'I'm sure it is,' Lieutenant Gamble said. 'If you hadn't gotten a flat tire, you'da

283

been in on the pinch,' Mac said. 'But that's police work. Rain today, snow tomorrow. Take him away, Lieutenant. Get his head patched up, and heave him in my lockup, or take him to headquarters with you.' He looked, for all the world, like a performing poodle.

'It occurs to me,' Lieutenant Gamble said, 'that the attorney general isn't going to be happy. Whoever has to prosecute Henry Lighton is going to have a bad time in court.'

'Not with a case that Otto McLane worked up,' Mac said. 'When I pinch them, they stay pinched. Now get him out of here. I got work to do. Andy can't run that feed-and-seed store, and I can't take my good factory job till I find her somebody who can. How's about it, Porter? If you was a dealer, you could give that yellow-bellied boss of yours some bad times. He's got it coming to him, running out on you when you was in trouble. Guys oughtn't to run out on a friend of Otto McLane's.'

All that occurred to me was that if my plans went the way I hoped they would, I was in for some bad times myself, if my children took after their grandfather.

THE MISTRESS OF EVIL

V. J. Banis

John Hamilton travels to the Carpathian Mountains in Romania, along with his wife Victoria and her sister Carolyn, to research the risk of earthquakes in the area. The government provides lodgings for them in the ancient Castle Drakul. Upon investigating a disused basement room, the trio discover a skeleton in a coffin with a wooden stake through its rib cage — and Carolyn feels a strange compulsion to goad John into removing it. Soon afterward, a sinister visitor arrives at the castle — claiming to be a descendant of the original Count Drakul . . .

THE GREEN MANDARIN MYSTERY

Denis Hughes

When a number of eminent scientists — all experts in their field, and of inestimable value to the British Government — mysteriously vanish, the police are at their wits' end. The only clue in each instance is a note left by the scientist saying they have joined 'the Green Mandarin'. Desperate to locate his daughter, Fleurette, a Home Office official enlists the services of scientific detective Ray Ellis. But as his investigations get closer to the truth, will Ray be the next person to go missing?

KNIGHT-ERRANT

Norman Firth

Lance Knight notices a beautiful woman with a notorious criminal in a London restaurant, who is clearly threatening her, and refers to her disparagingly as 'your majesty'. Knight decides to follow her when she leaves — and finds himself saving her after she deliberately throws herself in front of a bus! So begins his most dangerous adventure . . . And in *Passion's Victim*, June Mallory is determined to prove her father innocent of the burglary for which he was imprisoned — and is caught in a tangled web of betrayal and murder.

THE ROOT OF ALL EVIL

Valerie Holmes

When Bartholomew Denton, the owner of Leaham Hall in North Yorkshire, is discovered dead in his bed, Detection Officer Sergeant Hector Blagdon is called in. Young and fit as Denton was, the death seems suspicious. Blagdon is also intrigued by the quick turnover of maid-servants at the Hall, and wonders if there is something else going on. With his old adversary Kendel the butler seemingly trying to frustrate the investigation, Blagdon must delve deep to find answers . . .